W9-DBR-652

BE THAT
WAY
HOPE LARSON
MARGARET FERGUSON BOOKS
HOLIDAY HOUSE
NEW YORK

Margaret Ferguson Books

Printed and bound in June 2023 at Leo Paper, Heshan, China.
The art and lettering in this book were created using an iPad Pro,
Adobe Photoshop, and Adobe Illustrator.
www.holidayhouse.com
First Edition
1 3 5 7 9 10 8 6 4 2

Library of Congress Cataloging-in-Publication Data

Names: Larson, Hope, author.
Title: Be that way / by Hope Larson.
Description: First edition. | New York : Margaret Ferguson Books/Holiday House, [2023] | Audience: Ages 12 and up. | Audience: Grades 10–12.
Summary: Sixteen-year-old Christine keeps a journal of an eventful year of her life in mid-90s Asheville, North Carolina, which she records through prose and illustration.
Identifiers: LCCN 2022027040 | ISBN 9780823447619 (hardcover)
Subjects: CYAC: Graphic novels. | Diaries—Fiction.
LCGFT: Diary fiction. | Graphic novels.
Classification: LCC PZ7.7.L37 Be 2023 | DDC 741.5/973—dc23/eng/20220903
LC record available at https://lccn.loc.gov/2022027040

ISBN: 978-0-8234-4761-9 (hardcover)

The excerpt that appears on pg. 164 is from *Jane Eyre* by Charlotte Brontë.

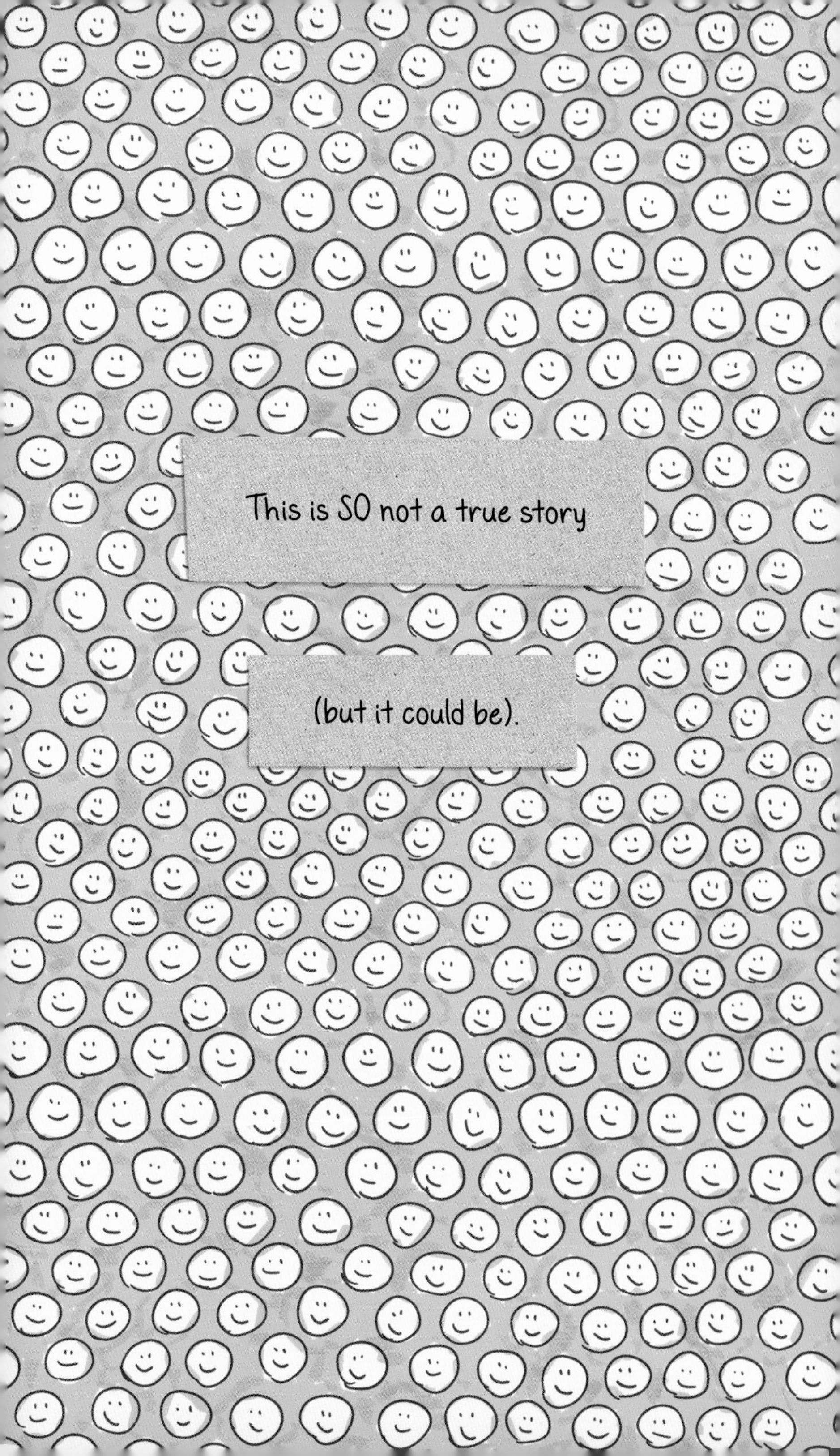
This is SO not a true story
(but it could be).

COMPOSITION
1993
200 pag
9¾ x 7½ inche

Friday, October 22nd, 1993

Dear Diary,

Hello. My name is Christine. I'm fourteen years old, I'm in ninth grade, and my teachers all think I'm messed up in the head. That's why I'm starting this journal.

What happened was, last month in art class I did this drawing of a girl with scars all over her arms. It wasn't even supposed to be me; I'd just read an article in Seventeen about girls who cut themselves, and I was trying to be edgy, or deep, or something. But my art teacher mentioned it to my English teacher, who was "concerned" because I'd written a "morbid" story for her class—which I thought she'd like since she assigns stuff like that old "Owl Creek Bridge" story where the protagonist gets murdered—and all of a sudden, there I was in the principal's office for an "emergency meeting" about my "cry for help." It was horrible: they called Mom at work, and she came in, and we both cried. No one should have to see their mom cry in the principal's office.

I was able to convince everyone that, yeah, my dad died, and yeah, I'm sad about it, but I'm not about to off myself. The guidance counselor—she was there, too—thought an extracurricular would help me get out of my head, and she suggested the Cougar Chronicle because they're always looking for writers. I was, like, fine, I'll write for the paper. I'll do anything to get you all off my back.

But it turns out I love writing for the Chronicle. I can go to the office whenever I have a free period, and there's always someone in there, hanging out. The first issue I worked on just came out, and it was cool to see my article in there. Mom was psyched, too.

I'm also learning to fly under the radar in my classes. Like, now I see that when they tell us to "be creative," they actually mean, "Make some bland, nonthreatening crap I can put on the bulletin board in the hall." Write an essay about the time your dog ate the Thanksgiving turkey. Draw Marvin the Martian, or leaping dolphins in front of a sunset, or Sinead O'Connor from the cover of Rolling Stone. Whatever—just be normal, like everyone else.

The funny thing is, trying so hard to be normal is starting to make me feel crazy. Like, if I don't empty out all the murky goop swishing around in my brain, my head will eventually explode. But I'm not about to upset Mom again, or get sent back to the principal, so I'll put it all here—every strange, secret part of myself that no one can ever know.

So? I already know all your secrets. And I'm the bad one, not you. Did I tell you I got detention today?

No! Why?

Jack was staring at my boobs so I threw a tampon at him.

A USED tampon?!

Ew, of course not! It's so annoying. They didn't even make him apologize. No wonder high school boys are so unevolved.

Ummm, that sucks, Landry, but this is a private space for Christine's Sad Girl Thoughts ONLY.

Until two weeks from now when you decide you're sick of journaling, like every other time you tried to keep a diary.

Whatever. Are you sleeping over tonight?

Can I? My parents are yelling a lot this week.

Sure. Mom's grief group is coming over, but she's going to rent Princess Bride and order a pizza for the kiddies and me.

Cool.

Great. Now give back my journal and KEEP OUT.

I want to bang Westley.
Shhhh!

1994
Eraser

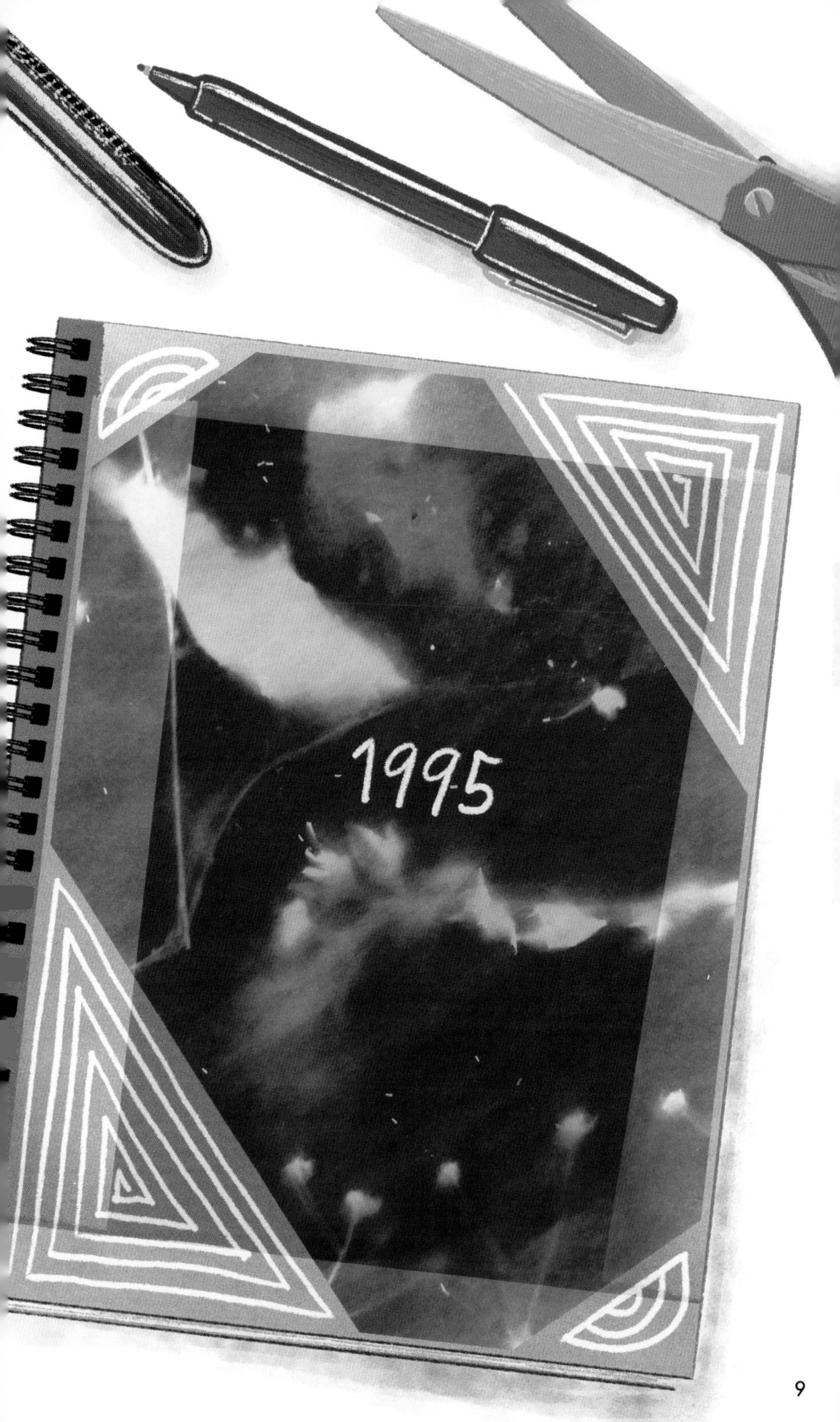

1995

KO-REX
CORRECTIVE

1996

zzz
SSSs

Wednesday, January 3rd, 1996
Asheville, NC

What's the cutoff date for New Year's resolutions? Do I still have time? Is there a point? I went back through my journals to see if I accomplished any of my resolutions from the last three years, and my success rate is zero. Also, now that I've reached the mature age of sixteen, it disturbs me that the main people invested in my self-improvement are Estée Lauder, Bobbi Brown, and whatever has-been actress is shilling for Weight Watchers this year. But I'm a good girl at heart, and I feel like I should resolve to do something, even if I don't follow through.

School started up again today and it's clear I have vacation brain rot. Mom was working third shift at the hospital, and I was supposed to make April and Brandon's lunches before I went to bed, but I forgot, so this morning I was scrambling. April almost missed her bus. I seriously don't get why anyone has kids. I like to think that when I'm Mom's age I'll be living in a garret in Paris, drinking espresso with my much younger lover, not frantically assembling cheese sandwiches.

Although, if I was smart, I'd forget the whole lover thing, too. If I could harness all the energy I spend thinking about guys, I could power the city for a week.

Last night I dreamed about Dave. We broke up a month ago—I broke up with HIM—and I don't miss him at all. He was boring, he took me for granted, and we were only together for a month, but for some reason my subconscious has yet to evict him. Most of me is like,

But there's this other part that says,

Maybe I really am afraid of being alone, which is a distinct possibility for someone like me, a dork who pairs low status with high standards. I've kissed other guys, but Dave was my only actual boyfriend. Unlike Landry, who's had so many paramours I can't remember them all.

Every guy who looks at Landry falls deeply in lust—except for Paul, who says,

He's right, but I'd be conceited, too, if I had hair down to my ass and legs up to my neck, and I literally turned heads walking around downtown. The heads of bums and burnouts, because that's who hangs out there, but still. She has this aura, this glow with no identifiable source that clings to her like radioactive dust. Maybe one day it'll rub off on me and I'll be shiny, too. For a brief moment I'll be that girl everyone wants and wants to be.

And then eventually my teeth will fall out and I'll die of radiation exposure. And my tombstone will read,

I get my share of looks from random guys, but it's probably because of my hair. Right now it's Burnt Raisin, and the color on the box is a mauve-y brown, but on my head it turned pinkish-purple. Maybe I left it on too long? Anyway, I like that it matches my Docs. Currently I have major roots and I'm trying to decide if I'll remain a Burnt Raisin girl or mix it up again.

I know it doesn't really matter—no hair dye on Earth could make me as incandescent as Landry—but in photos of us when we were five, or eight, or ten, we don't look that different. I may not have as much to work with, but this year I'm going to make an effort. I'm going to be the kind of girl that people notice.

New Year's Resolution, 1996:

BE SHINY!

(And get a new boyfriend. ☺)

Friday, January 5th

Paul tried to get a group together to see 12 Monkeys at the Mall Twin, but no one else cares about Terry Gilliam. I do, but I'm watching the kiddies tonight because Mom has work. And I don't have a car (yet). And I'm broke.

Paul and I have been writing for the Cougar Chronicle since ninth grade. We've had classes together, too, but we didn't really hang out at school until this year, because Landry and I coordinated our schedules and I was always with her. Now that she's going to her fancy private school, Paul's become my surrogate best friend at Asheville High. His girlfriend, Jennifer—not Jen: JennIFER—hates me, so that complicates things, but I can mostly avoid her since she has a different lunch period than Paul and me. Her Love's Baby Soft is always with us, though, clinging to Paul's clothes like a cloying, bitchy specter.

Landry's theory is that JennIFER's afraid I'll steal her man, but I don't buy it. She hated me even when I was going out with Dave—who is good friends with Paul. He and I don't talk about Dave. We have an implicit understanding that it would be too awkward.

Besides, I don't like Paul that way. And even if I did, if we dated and broke up, who would make fun of everyone else with me? Who else at the Cougar Chronicle would I talk to about Harold and Maude and The X-Files? He's not my physical type, either. The dudes I lust after are preps, which is...not Paul.

PAUL

Diagram of a Dude

Just tall enough to not be short.

Always goes too long between haircuts.

Wears these stupid bowling shirts every freaking day. He must have a dozen.

And he listens to jazz. I mean, he's basically middle-aged.

I think Paul's with JennIFER because she's an actress and he wants her to be in his movie. If he ever gets the script done. He's a good writer, but every time I finish reading a draft, he tells me to forget it because he's had "a better idea" and started the whole cycle over again. He's rewritten it three times since September.

Saturday, January 6th

It's snowing! We already had two inches when I woke up. I went out into the snow that no one had walked in yet and felt guilty for messing it up because I wasn't even going anywhere important; I was just sick of being inside. But if I hadn't done it, someone else would've. Is that a good enough reason for ruining something perfect?

It was so quiet I could hear flakes landing on the hood of my coat. Then, when I got to Grove Park, there was a dog running circles in the snow. I saw Reggie, the dog, before I saw Whit Godwin, the boy. The snow must have covered their tracks.

Whit looked over at me, and I don't know what came over me, but I waved. He waved back, and then we both pretended it hadn't happened.

It's not that I dislike him. Not overtly, anyway.

From the front, our houses look basically the same, but our backyards are where the truth comes out.
Check out my family's rusty swing set, kiddie-pool swamp, and lush poison ivy vines.

Then cross the alley and feast your eyes upon the Godwins' resort-like pool and teak lounge chairs. Thirsty? There's a fully stocked mini-fridge in the cabana.

We weren't always the rusty swing set people. We used to have vacations every summer, and name-brand groceries, and the Godwins came to our barbecues. Then Dad died, and Mom had to go back to working as a nurse, and the neighbors gradually got tired of feeling sorry for us and started ignoring us instead. I wish Mom would sell the house and move us to a cheaper neighborhood, but she always says she's too busy to look for a new place, or she wants us to all have our own rooms. Excuses. I think she's attached to it because it reminds her of how things used to be, which isn't exactly healthy.

Monday, January 8th

By Sunday afternoon we had a foot of snow. School was canceled and I wasn't on babysitting duty since Mom was off work, so I walked the two blocks to Landry's house and spent the night.

Landry's room looks nothing like her. Her mom had it professionally decorated and it's very purple. Everything from the walls to the carpet is lavender, mauve, or white. There are, like, fifteen pillows on the bed and she's not even allowed to put up posters.

Two years ago, when Landry was fourteen and obsessed with Nirvana, she made a secret collage of them on the back of her closet door. We did a séance in there and tried to contact Kurt Cobain with a Ouija board. Then I tried to reach my dad and spooked myself and knocked over a candle. Her mom saw the burn mark on the carpet and Landry got in trouble—even though it was in the closet, which, like, who cares?—but she never admitted it was my fault.

It's weird to think about, because for the past year, Landry's parents have been so checked out we could burn the house down without them noticing. They go to "Xambia" every night, which is what they call knocking themselves out with Xanax and Ambien.

Before Landry got her license in September (after failing twice), we'd sneak out and walk around our neighborhood in the middle of the night. Now, unless there's a party, we drive to Wendy's and flirt with the cute drive-through guy. Last night the roads were icy, so we walked to the golf course to sled. The snow had a crust of ice and we did these long, fast rides. I went into a ditch and screamed, and someone came out of a house yelling that they'd called the cops, so we left.

I took a rose-scented bubble bath in Landry's private bathroom and listened to her talk on the phone with someone named Corinne about someone named Marcellus. Everyone at her new school has a name like that and lives in a mansion. Landry claims they all suck, but when she rolled her eyes and told me a lot of her new friends had gone cross-country skiing together—they're too sophisticated to sled, like us—I could tell how much she wished they'd invited her, too. The only one of Landry's new school friends I've met was Juliet. She slept over with us one time and seemed cool, but two weeks later her parents separated and she moved to Florida with her mom.

I asked Landry what her New Year's resolution is, and she said she "doesn't believe in them." Of course she doesn't.

I lied and told her I didn't make one, either.

Tuesday, January 9th

I woke up to more snow and a fever. Mom gave me ibuprofen and Gatorade, told me to call if I "really need to," and went to work. Landry's sick, too—I guess we caught it from each other—and she called to tell me she "accidentally" got high on cough syrup and I should try it because if I got caught I'd have plausible deniability.

Since it was another snow day, I was stuck watching Brandon and April. I tried to make them go play in the snow so I could be sick in peace, but they stayed inside and fought over the TV remote. I quarantined myself in my room, taped songs off the radio, and read old issues of Sassy. Writing for them must be the coolest. The girls who do all sound like the kind of person I want to be: smart, funny, worldly. They reviewed a bunch of new lipstick colors with names like Rouge Vampire and Co-ed Coral, and I wish I was the kind of girl who "mixes it up," but I'm committed to my Black Honey lipstick.

I just realized that my lips, hair, and shoes are all purple or mauve. It's like I subconsciously decorated myself to match Landry's room.

I went through my closet and tried on stuff I haven't worn lately, hoping to unearth a forgotten gem, but all I accomplished was hating my body and despairing of ever being shiny. All my cute vintage dresses are disintegrating and my favorite baggy jeans are ripping in the butt—and even if they weren't, grunge isn't cool anymore. My allowance won't cover an entire new wardrobe, and I can't get a job because Mom depends on me to babysit, so my only option is to wear the clothes I have until they literally fall in pieces from my body. Maybe when I have to start wearing a bedsheet toga to school Mom will let me seek gainful employment.

Friday, January 12th

We had snow for the rest of the week, which is really weird for Asheville, and everything's still shut down and I'm still sick and the walls are closing in. But hey, I'm not the only one losing it. I saw Whit Godwin jog by in shorts. SHORTS! In the snow!

I've been missing Dave—but only in a very compartmentalized way. Like how great he was on the phone. He'd talk about anything and he'd stay on the line forever. The most romantic experience I had with him was when we fell asleep talking and "slept together" on the phone—it was somehow more romantic and intimate than making out with him.

I called Landry to talk about Dave, and she told me to just forget about him because he's a jerk and why do I even bother with high school boys, anyway? I should "move on" like she has so I can date someone "worthwhile," which for her means boys in college. I just need to "put myself out there." I snapped that our puritanical society doesn't approve of women putting themselves out there and she "got a call on the other line" and "had to go."

Whatever. If she won't listen to me bitch about feminism, she doesn't get to hear my thoughts on Whit Godwin's surprisingly attractive legs.

Sunday, January 14th

The snow's finally melting and Mom had an uncharacteristic urge to go to church, which meant we all had to go. Bleh, but at least we got out of the house. After the service I snarfed down a dozen of those little round shortbreads with jam in the middle while Mom got swarmed by prehistoric church ladies demanding to know where we'd been for three years. I could tell from Mom's face that she was remembering why we stopped coming.

Afterward we drove straight to McDonald's for Happy Meals and spent the afternoon playing Monopoly. Brandon kept landing in jail, I went bankrupt, April cried, and Mom kicked all our asses.

Monday, January 15th

For the first time in a week, the sun came out, and just riding the bus to school was like a party. I felt so good that I said hi to Dave when I saw him in the hall. He walked right by me, so he must still be mad.

I think the teachers were happy to be back, too, except for Ms. Saylor. While we were talking about One Flew Over the Cuckoo's Nest I accidentally referenced something in a later chapter, and she lectured me about how I'm "hampering" class discussion by reading ahead and how Honors English isn't about reading fast, it's about reading thoroughly.

I like her class—and Paul's in it, too—but the way we treat books is seriously messed up. We chloroform them and cut them open and look at the strange tender organs that make them live, and in the process, kill 'em dead. What kind of way is that to act toward something beautiful?

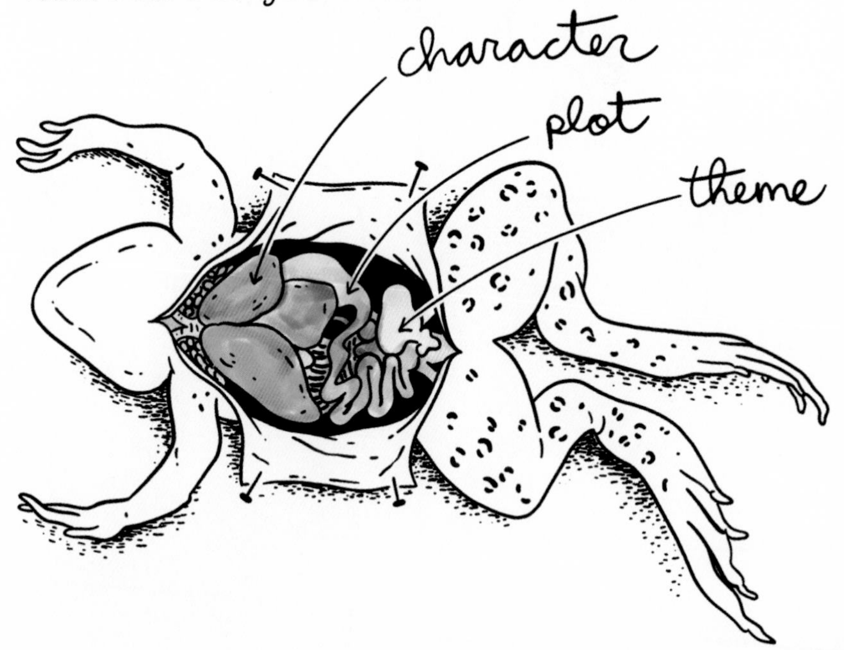

I'm glad I'm a journalist, not a novelist, because no one's going to eviscerate my article about the prom committee's bake sale in a search for its underlying meaning. I tried talking to Paul about it at lunch but all he wanted to talk about was his screenplay.

POOF
Hey, babe.
Hey!
Speak of the devil!

What's up, JennIFER?
Leaving early. I have an audition in Greenville.
BRUSH
PRIMP

Cool. What for?
A commercial. Instant oatmeal.
GLOSS

Bland and prepackaged?
Sounds perfect for you.
Yeah.

So, could you, like, go away?

Paul has to help me run lines.
Right. No prob. Break a leg!

Or both.

Friday, January 19th

Landry wanted to see some jam band at Be Here Now, so I told Mom we were going to the movies and having a sleepover at her house. Then the hospital called and offered Mom an extra shift, and I was like, shit, I'll have to stay home. But she decided I could still go out if Landry slept over at our house instead, and we were home by 11:30. She made a big deal out of leaving Brandon in charge. Why?! He's twelve! I started babysitting the kiddies when I was eleven.

Landry drove us downtown in her '83 Mercedes—her family's version of a beater car—and the guy checking IDs at the door let us in even though he totally knew ours were fake. The opening band was already playing and the room was a crush of standard-issue locals. White dude with dreads and BO—check. Cool girl in striped knee-high socks from Interplanet Janet—check. Sad boy who haunts Downtown Books & News—check.

I'd used a new shampoo and my hair smelled really great and I was feeling shiny, for once, so naturally some guy spilled his beer on my shirt the second we got to the dance floor. He started yelling, I started crying, and Landry shoved me toward the bathroom to get cleaned up while she dealt with him. By the time I got back, covered in pilled-up bits of T.P. because they were out of paper towels, Landry was dancing with Angry Yelling Beer Guy. When I went over, he smiled and apologized, and I realized I know him. Kind of.

His name's Jason, and he was a senior at Asheville High when we were freshmen. He used to be this clean-cut football player everyone had a crush on, even though he always seemed kind of stupid, like he caught too many balls to the head. He's even hotter now that he's grown his hair long, and he's tall—at least 6'2".

While Landry did her whole predictable mating ritual, I drifted off and tucked myself into a shadowy corner. I watched the flannel shirts and baby-doll dresses circling, flirting, getting sloppier and stupider the more they drank. I know my resolution is to be someone people notice, but sometimes it's more fun to be a voyeur.

Landry gave me the rundown in the car, which I drove since she was buzzed off all the sips she took from Jason's beer. She remembered him, too. He goes to school at App State, but he comes home a lot to see friends. He's studying meteorology. He asked for her number, so she wrote it on his arm. I've seen her use that trick before.
Now we're home and Landry's snoring on my pillow with her makeup on. Even asleep, she looks perfect.

Wednesday, January 24th

The library screened The Big Sleep tonight, for free, and Paul said I should go. Even though it was a school night, Mom and Brandon and April ended up coming, too, but they found seats on the other side of the room to give me some space. I sat with Paul and JennIFER and was afraid nobody else was going to come. When Paul went to the bathroom and left us alone for a minute, I asked JennIFER if she got the oatmeal commercial. She rolled her eyes and said she didn't want to talk about it, so we sat in semi-silence until (thank God) Kayla showed up.

Kayla's really Paul's friend, but she's in my trig class and she writes for the Chronicle. Last year she wrote this great piece for the Halloween issue about how her backyard butts up against Riverside Cemetery and she once saw a ghost. Pretty sure it wasn't true, but I want to believe.

After the movie, everyone discussed Humphrey Bogart's sex appeal, which can be summed up as sad eyes and short ties. We all cringed when JennIFER said that Paul's kind of a Bogie type, because why would you tell your boyfriend you think he's ugly-hot? I think Paul saw me roll my eyes at Kayla, but he deserves so much better than JennIFER.

Friday, February 2nd

Without fail, February packs the most bullshit into the fewest number of days. I feel less shiny than ever and it doesn't help that tomorrow is...you know.

Landry gets that this time of year is hard for me, so she came over before her date with Jason (of course he asked her out) to help me dye my hair and cheer me up. The plan was for me to go red—an almost-found-in-nature hue called Copper Light—but we didn't strip out all the Burnt Raisin so there are random splotches all over my head. ☹

We spent a long time laughing about how all the adjectives on the box of dye are blatantly sexual.

Saturday, February 3rd

Missing you today, Dad. I drew this from my favorite photo of you. Didn't totally nail the likeness, but I know you'd forgive me.

Wednesday, February 14th

Valentine's Day: yet another thing to hate about this stupid month. The lovey vibes floating around school were suffocating, and at lunch Paul and I got in a fight about my bad attitude re: JennIFER, so I spent the rest of the time with the art kids, getting high out of an apple in the woods behind Enth. That's what Landry and I call the Ear Nose Throat Head doctor next door to the school.

We talked about how we're hung up on lame commercial holidays like this because culture is dead and there's nothing important happening in the world. Every other generation got a defining moment, like a war, but the '90s is a decade of inertia.

By the time the bell rang I was feeling okay, but when I was on my way to PE, Paul swooped in next to me to "clear the air." I was like, fine, let's get it over with, and he was like,

That stopped me. He doesn't know Landry like I do. She can be self-absorbed, but she's also the girl whose parents give her cash for every birthday because they have no clue what her interests are. Whose dad got drunk at the neighborhood picnic and made a scene. Whose mom once threatened to send her to the "fat farm." I couldn't tell him that stuff, of course. I keep her secrets and she keeps mine.

For Paul's sake I'm going to make an effort with JennIFER.

Saturday, February 17th

I was supposed to have school today. It was scheduled as a makeup day for all the snow days we had last month, but...it got snowed out. Now they're talking about cutting into spring break, which sucks, but in the moment I am happy to be free.

Landry and I risked death on the supposedly icy (but perfectly safe) roads to spend the afternoon at the mall with some of the girls from her school.

Landry was excited—but also mopey because Jason canceled their date tonight. His car doesn't have four-wheel drive and he didn't want to drive to Asheville in the snow, but she's convinced herself the real reason is he doesn't want to see her anymore. She has insane confidence when it comes to landing guys, but once she's got them, a switch flips and she gets incredibly insecure.

We dissected her convo with Jason, syllable by syllable, until we met up with the girls outside Journeys. It was a big group—eight, including us—and we rolled through the mall together like a teen girl version of The Blob. Old people were practically diving into Yankee Candle to get out of our path.

Everyone was nice to me. Corinne told me she loved my hair and wished she could dye hers, too, but their school has a strict dress code. They must not care about piercings, though, because she had three little gold studs in each ear. I thought she was cool and we could be friends—her, Landry, and me.

Landry had worked herself into a manic state, which she does sometimes when she's nervous, and when we got to the Gap, she said we should pick out clothes for each other and do a fashion show. I tried to do my fade-into-the-background thing while everyone else strutted up and down the fitting room aisle, but Landry was determined to include me, and I told myself Shiny Christine would be game.

Here's what Landry picked for me to model:

Everyone said I HAD to get the skirt 'cause it was SO me—although they just met me, so how would they know?—and plus it was on sale! It felt like destiny, but when I got to the register, it turned out I'd done the math wrong and I was a few dollars short. Embarrassing, but I was relieved. I shouldn't have let myself get peer-pressured into spending so much money when I'm saving to get my own car. I was telling the cashier I'd put everything back so she wouldn't have to bother when Landry tapped my shoulder and handed me five bucks.

That's okay. I'll get it some other time.

But it's the last one! It's on sale!
It...
It's really okay.

Come on! You HAVE to get it!

I don't HAVE to do ANYthing!
eep!

OooOooo.

I hadn't meant to yell, but I couldn't understand why Landry kept pushing me. She got really quiet, and after the rest of the Girl-Blob left to see a movie, she laid into me.

Sorry for getting mad at me? Or sorry for herself?

We were supposed to go to Beanstreets for coffee, but after our fight, neither of us was in the mood. Before we even left the parking lot, Landry slid on black ice and almost rear-ended some old dude's sedan. She was so upset I had to drive us home.

I'm not angry with her, exactly, but I feel like garbage. I'm not going to call her for a while.

Friday, February 23rd

When I got home from school, Mom's annoying friend Eileen was camped out in our living room, trying to sell Mom a bunch of essential oils and aromatherapy junk, which is her latest side business. I wasn't up for sitting through the sales pitch so I booked it to my room and hid.

When I was thinking about calling Landry, the phone rang. She was calling me! We must have been on the same witchy wavelength.

She'd just been to the Goddess Store. It felt shitty that she'd gone without me—like, she's not allowed to avoid ME! I'm the one avoiding HER. Then she told me she'd bought me a tarot deck, and I felt shitty for feeling shitty.

She also got a book about Wicca for herself, and she kept me on the phone while she cast an attraction spell to keep Jason from falling out of love with her—although she says she's not really worried anymore, because he was in town Wednesday and took her out for coffee after school.

I was staring out the window while she talked and saw Whit Godwin bring the trash out and smoke a joint in the alley. It kind of shocked me. He's the practice-piano-every-afternoon type, not the smoking-in-the-alley type. For years, when I got home from school, weird piano medleys of pop songs would be floating out the window. But now that I think about it, it's been a long time since I heard him play.

Sunday, March 3rd

Mom and I are waiting for Brandon and April to be done at soccer practice. We're eating croissants at Old Europe, which is where we come when we want to feel fancy. Beanstreets will always be my go-to coffee place, but sometimes you aren't in the mood to hang out in a grunge hole covered in bad art and dismembered mannequin parts.

Mom's reading The Mists of Avalon, which she borrowed from essential-oils Eileen. (Eileen loves it, but Mom says it's too New Age for her.) We're at a table in the back room, away from the door, because we're both always cold.

Before she got her book out she went into nostalgia mode and told me for the one millionth time about escaping small-town Indiana to go to college in Chicago, meeting Dad, and their honeymoon in Paris, which was the first and only time she's been out of the country.

People always assumed they met at work, since lots of doctors marry nurses, but they were in the same undergrad biology class. Dad grew up in California and had a tan and long hair like a surf bum, so she thought he was going to be a dummy.

They should have been together forever, but because the arc of the universe bends toward suckiness, Mom's sitting here alone, reading a weird feminist fantasy novel.

Holy shit. Jason just sat down across from us. Landry's Jason. And he's with a girl who's a less-pretty version of Landry. Maybe her attraction spell backfired. He's in town, but he's with someone else.

He looked right at me and right THROUGH me. That's right, dude—my superpower is invisibility to hot assholes and I'm going to BRING YOU DOWN.

Waiting
at counter.
Un-Landry
GRRR!

Later.

I called Landry as soon as we got home. She didn't pick up, so I paged her beeper, but she didn't call back. Then I called every fifteen minutes until her dad picked up her private line and told me to STOP CALLING, CHRISTINE.

I redirected my anxiety into alphabetizing all my books, which led to the discovery of a fossilized bag of Twizzlers I squirreled away behind my Sweet Valley High collection in, like, 1993. When Landry finally called, it turned out she'd been at the movies with the cheater himself.

He went straight from coffee with his mystery blonde to Happy Gilmore with Landry. I wanted to tell her he's a two-timing dog, but before I could she started talking about what a great time they had. He bought her popcorn and held her hand for the whole movie.

She was so happy I couldn't force the words out. The truth is too cruel. I'll have to find another time to tell her.

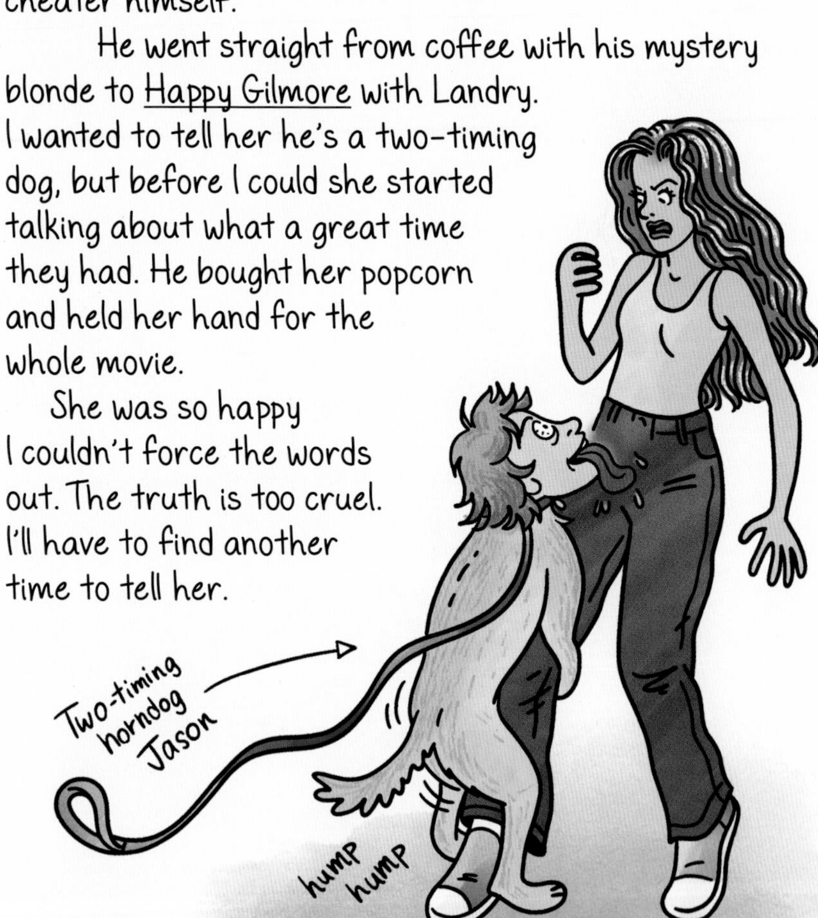

Thursday, March 7th

We started The Bell Jar in English. I probably shouldn't aspire to be like a lady who put her head in an oven, but Sylvia Plath was cool, smart, and pretty, and had my dream job at a magazine in New York City.

We had the sort of intense discussion Ms. Saylor's always hoping for, with the guys in class saying Plath was whiny and "not that smart" and all the girls calling them misogynists. A riot grrrl got so worked up she cried, and Paul was the only dude willing to defend Plath's talent.

I don't know how such a cool, smart guy came out of his family. He doesn't talk about them much, but I know his parents are the type who should divorce already and his brother has issues, too.

He told me their dog, Pepper, got out of the yard last night, and instead of going out to look for her, everyone but Paul got in a screaming match about who left the gate open. Paul spent an hour walking around, calling for Pepper while it got darker and colder, but she didn't come back.

He works at a sub sandwich place after school, so he cut last period to look for her. I went, too. All I had was study hall, and I didn't mind skipping that. I pretended to be disappointed that JennIFER was otherwise engaged, but he didn't buy it.

We drove around and listened to Thelonious Monk, which I actually liked, even though I prefer music with words. My favorite song was called "Suburban Eyes." A perfect title.

It was my first time in his car, an old Corolla that smelled like stale coffee and boy funk. The seats and dashboard were vaguely grimy, but there wasn't any trash on the floor. He doesn't leave anything inside because, in his neighborhood, people will break your window to steal spare change out of your cup holder. I wonder if his room is like this, too. Does it have the same odor? Does he make his bed?

As we drove, the jazz in the background made everything feel like an indie movie about teenage ennui: scads of atmosphere, zero plot.

I asked Paul what to do about Landry and Jason and he thinks I should tell her in person, not on the phone. I'm sleeping over at her house tomorrow, so I'll do it then.

We didn't find Pepper, but Paul called after dropping me at home and said she'd come back on her own. While we were out looking, she was curled up in her bed with a belly full of Snausages.

Paul and I are, like, 10% better friends than we were this morning. Life is weird.

Saturday, March 9th

As a thank-you, Paul made me a tape of his favorite jazz songs, including "Suburban Eyes." I played it for Landry last night and she smirked and said, "You finally stole him from JennIFER?"

I rolled my eyes and told her it was because I helped him look for his dog. I'd never "steal" a guy from someone. That's so trashy. And then, because I was worked up, I barfed out what I'd been wanting to tell her all week:

URP.
So? Maybe they're friends.

No way.

How do you know?

Because I have EYES! Look, I drew them! Judge for yourself.

I don't need to. He's allowed.

Allowed to CHEAT on you?!

We're DATING, Christine, not GOING OUT.

I can't believe she's making excuses for him. I get the third degree over a dumb tape and Jason gets to sit in coffee shops and play footsie with random chicks, no questions asked? I don't get it.

She did at least admit it's time they had the boyfriend/girlfriend talk. I suggested she cut her losses and dump him, but she thinks if I spent time with them I'll see how good they are together. Like I don't have better things to do than shadow her on her dates!

Thursday, March 14th

It was 70 degrees today. At lunch everyone was laid out on the grass, high on vitamin D, bodies on display for the first time in months. The horniness was palpable.

On my way to the bus I glanced over and saw Dave making out with a sophomore in patchwork jeans. I knew this would happen sooner or later, and I'd been banking on later, but I didn't even feel jealous.

He looked over and saw me, and I smiled, and he smiled back.

Landry called and said Jason had invited her to a party tomorrow night and she wanted me to come, too. When I said yes right away, she seemed surprised. She probably thought she'd have to talk me into it, but Shiny Christine is ready to see and be seen and P-A-R-T-Y! This is St. Paddy's Day weekend, and I'm part Irish on Mom's side, so maybe I'll get lucky.

Plus I'd feel guilty not going. If she went without me and something happened, it might be days before her parents even noticed she was gone.

I got permission to spend the night at Landry's. I obviously couldn't tell Mom we were going to a party with a college guy; she's constantly telling me stories about girls coming to the ER after getting roofied, and how glad she is that she "doesn't need to worry" about me.

Saturday, March 16th

Last night was like, whoa.

Jason picked me and Landry up from her house. He was driving a dented Taurus and his friend Tod was riding shotgun. Landry offered to sit in back with me, but Jason said absolutely not; she's his "lady." Tod was obviously pissed about having to sit in back, but Jason assured him that I'm cool, which is rich coming from the guy who didn't recognize me at the coffee shop.

Tod smelled like cigarettes and mildew and looked sort of...weathered. He creeped me out, so I reframed the situation as an opportunity to work on my skills as an interviewer.

That was the last thing he said to me, so I just sat there and watched Jason's right hand creep along Landry's thigh, closer and closer to her crotch. That must be the kind of "we're good together" stuff she wanted me to see.

The party was in an abandoned warehouse in the wasteland below downtown, between the train tracks and the river—a crumbling temple lost in a kudzu jungle. There weren't any streetlights, and when I got out of the car I felt like we were a million miles from everything. It felt dangerous, but just enough to be exciting.

A group of college students was smoking outside. They waved to Tod, who speed-walked off to join them, and I saw him palm something into someone's hand. Everything clicked: he was there to sell drugs. I was dying to tell Landry but I didn't want to shit-talk Jason's friend right in front of him.

Inside the warehouse, a DJ was spinning techno on a plywood platform. I think the party was supposed to be a rave, but it wasn't like the ones I'd heard about in Charlotte and Atlanta. There were two girls dressed up in body glitter and candy necklaces, but otherwise it was the same people in the same kind of clothes as anywhere else in town, and not enough of them to keep the room from feeling empty. There was a keg of green beer and Jason brought us each a cup, then Landry did her usual thing and dragged him off to dance and left me alone. I threw out my beer after one sip. It had a putrid taste, like river water.

Eventually someone fired up a smoke machine, and it started to feel like a party. The room felt less empty, anyway, and it no longer mattered that I didn't know anyone. We were all anonymous silhouettes dancing in the chemical fog.

A face emerged from the smoke next to me, and I recognized a boy from school. He was tall and skinny with blue hair, a pierced eyebrow, baggy pants, and a T-shirt that hung to his knees. Little by little we went from dancing NEAR each other to dancing WITH each other.

I was totally mesmerized by the flashing lights glinting off his eyebrow ring and his beautiful clear gray eyes.

He said something I couldn't hear, and I nodded, because I wanted to seem like I was up for anything. He pulled me over to the wall and I was sure he was going to kiss me, but instead he reached into the pocket of his giant raver pants and pulled out a bottle of water.

He handed it to me and I drank it without thinking, then panicked because what if I'd just been roofied?! But he drank some, too, so I figured it was fine.

His name was Peace, which is the best my-parents-were-hippies name I've heard. He came to the party with a friend, a college girl he works with at the Ingles deli, but she bumped into an ex and went off with him. My heart leaped because that probably meant Peace was single! I told myself that he DID want to kiss me but he was still working up the confidence. But when he looked out at the dance floor, he complained that there weren't any hot guys.

So, Peace is single, but gay. Oops.

Then Landry came barreling over.

CHRISTIIINE! I'M SOOO WASTED!
God, how?! That beer is nasty!

Jason has a flask.
Giggle

Of course. And where is he now?

Um...

I don't know.

He got you drunk and left you alone? Cool. Great guy.

He's gone off with some other girl, hasn't he?

No, no, I don't think—

SOB!
I have to find him!
Shit.

Landry, WAIT!

I said goodbye to Peace and chased after Landry. Jason wasn't with Tod and the other smokers, which made her freak out even more. Then she bolted across the road. She ran over the railroad tracks toward the river, pulling off her fuzzy sweater and shouting that she was going to drown herself. I stumbled after her through knee-high weeds (which ripped my last good pair of tights), wondering how she'd gotten so far ahead, when she tripped on an old tire hidden in the grass and went down hard. I helped her put her sweater back on and sat on the tire rubbing her back while she bawled, and picked the burrs off her clothes and convinced her it was time to go home.

It pisses me off when she gets like this—drunk and making drama out of nothing—but I try to be patient. I was hard to be around when Dad died, but she stayed with me. I owe her.

We saw Peace in the parking lot and, since Jason was still MIA, he offered to take us home, but the second we climbed into his little '70s hatchback—blue, like his hair—there was Jason, storming over with his alpha male chest puffed out. I didn't want Peace to get his ass kicked, so I explained Landry was sick and we had to leave NOW.

Jason grumbled that he'd drive us. I knew he'd been drinking, and who knew what else, but I was too scared to tell him no. Peace asked if I was sure and I just nodded, and Landry and I got out of his car.

Jason took us on a crazy drive on an almost-one-lane road that wound up the hill from the river. He was going way too fast, and every time we rounded a curve I expected headlights to leap out of the dark and send us to oblivion, "Leader of the Pack"-style. At the top of the hill he parked to show us the view. I just wanted to get back to Landry's, but it WAS pretty up there. Below us was the big bridge over the river, and to the west was Patton Ave., where cars of teens were cruising in circles past Denny's and Burger King. Overhead were stars, and stars, and stars.

Jason must have forgotten I was there, because he put his hand under Landry's sweater. She wasn't having it, so he sighed and started the car again. When he glanced in the rearview mirror and saw me watching, his face turned ugly.

No one said a word until we got into town and Jason mumbled something about Landry wasting his time. She blew up, screamed at him for playing the field, for cheating on her. The two of them were yelling back and forth, and then she started hitting him. While he was driving! I screamed as he went right through a red light and just barely missed getting T-boned.

He pulled over and told us to get the hell out. I did. Landry wouldn't. Jason took out a ten and told her to call a cab. She still didn't move, so I yanked her out of the car. Jason threw the cash out the window and drove away.

We were downtown, a couple miles from Landry's house. The night city is magical when you're safe in a car, but when you're on foot, it's different. I felt exposed, and our footsteps seemed so loud. Every time we passed a pay phone I tried to call a cab, but the phones were all broken. There were sirens far away, and whenever I saw a person in the distance I tensed up. But it still wasn't as scary as being in Jason's car.

We were almost to Landry's when we passed the little stone church by Grove Park. She wanted to go in and warm up, and I told her it wouldn't be open in the middle of the night, but she tried the door and it was unlocked. It was cozy inside and smelled like incense. We sat in a pew and held hands and leaned against each other. Her sweater was soft against my arm, except for the scratchy tip of a burr I'd missed.

I woke up a few hours later. It was getting light outside the stained-glass windows. I nudged Landry awake and we walked the rest of the way to her house. We crawled into her big, soft, pastel bed and slept until noon.

Tuesday, March 19th

Mom was at work and I was on kiddie patrol, and Landry walked over after school to study and eat chocolate. She said she's officially single again since Jason hasn't called her, but I think it was pretty official when he abandoned us downtown in the middle of the night.

On top of the nice-high-school-boy proclamation, she wants to get her GPA up before applying to colleges. We're both taking AP U.S. History, so we'd agreed she'd come over more so we can study together and keep each other on track.

Sometimes Landry reminds me of Pluto, which has a tilted orbit and plays by different rules than the other planets. When she's single she's closer to me than anyone, and when she's with a guy she drifts so far away I need a telescope.

Friday, March 22nd

For two weeks, Brandon's been obsessed with Chrono Trigger, this Nintendo game he borrowed from a friend. He's always been territorial about the TV, but now he's monopolizing the phone, too. Every time he gets stuck he calls James for help, and then they stay on the line while Brandon tries to beat the boss or solve the puzzle he's stuck on. It's kept him out of my hair, so I haven't really minded, but today was the day I ran out of patience. April was bored and whining, and I was trying to graph the function f(x)=sin(x), and I told Brandon he had to let her play, too.

It wasn't long before I heard them yelling, then a loud thud, and when I got there they'd knocked over the couch! I pulled them apart and told them to go to their rooms, but Brandon screamed that April ruined his game and I'm a power-tripping bitch and ran out the back door.

After an hour I made April put a coat on and come with me to look for him. We found him kickboxing a tree in Sunset Park and I lured him home by promising to make peanut butter blossoms with my secret stash of Hershey's Kisses. That ended up being what we ate for dinner.

When Mom got home I told her what happened, and as a fellow candy hoarder she fully grokked the sacrifice I'd made. Later, she slid an envelope under the door.

Wednesday, March 27th

Landry and I were studying at my kitchen table when a basketball flew over the fence and just missed landing in the kiddie pool, where last fall's leaves had decomposed into sludge. This tall, cute guy I'd never seen came after it, strolling through our yard like he had every right to be there. Landry knew him from her school so we went out to say hi.

His name's Eric. He invited us to join the pickup game he and Whit were playing in the alley—Whit was hovering at the edge of the yard, probably aware he wasn't welcome—but Landry and I are both pretty bad at sports, so instead we hung around and talked. Eric and Landry did, anyway; they're the same shiny-type person and they were really vibing. I asked how Whit and Eric know each other, and Whit said their dads are partners at the same law firm and they'd known each other since preschool. After that, neither of us had anything else to say. Eventually Landry said we had homework to finish and we'd see them around.

She claims she doesn't have a crush on Eric because "he has a girlfriend," but when has that stopped her? The whole time she was reading her history book she had a sneaky little smile on her face that said, "I've got him where I want him."

Tuesday, April 2nd

I thought Landry was into Eric, but she was only flirting with him to make Whit pay attention. And it worked; he called her last night to talk. She told me yesterday and I was like, "Oh, haha, April Fool's!"

But no. It's for real.

I don't know if Whit is technically a nice guy, but he's an order of magnitude nicer than her usual fare, especially Jason.

(But I wish she'd pick a nice high school guy who doesn't have an awkward history with me.)

(And I wish she'd stop jumping from boy to boy like they're rocks she has to balance on so she doesn't drown.)

Saturday, April 6th

Landry picked me up to go see Fargo at Hollywood Cinema and it wasn't till Whit was walking toward her car that she told me she "kind of accidentally" invited him along. And as if it wasn't bad enough to be the surprise third wheel with one set of friends, when we got to the theater, Paul waved to me from the next row, where he was sitting with JennIFER. Does that mean I was actually, like, a fifth wheel?

Whit and Landry talked about college. Landry doesn't know where she wants to go, but Whit's dad went to Yale so it's, like, a given he'll get in. Landry tried to draw me into their convo by telling me how much Whit and I have in common—how he wants to be a writer and I've been keeping a journal for years.

I kind of agree, but I tried so hard to not roll my eyes that I think I pulled a muscle.

On the ride home, Whit told us how his dad was the prosecuting attorney in the case of a guy who killed his girlfriend by pushing her off the side of a mountain. He was definitely guilty, but there wasn't enough proof to convinct so he got away with it. That kind of thing is why he'd never want to be a lawyer. His dad works for years on cases that get decided by the whims of a jury, and all he has to show for it is money. If you write books you don't make much money, but at least when you spend years on a book you have something to show for it.

Now I'm sitting in my room, in the dark, and I can see light through the curtains of Whit's room. I wonder what it's like inside. What's he doing right now?

Jerking off? Painting ducks? He's NOT writing in a journal. That's the one thing I know for sure.

Monday, April 8th

After school I saw Whit walking Reggie. He waved. I waved back. A lot's changed since January. Landry said he's asked her out for next Saturday.

Wednesday, April 10th

Paul loved Fargo so much he saw it again on Sunday. He's reviewing it for the Cougar Chronicle but the review's way longer than it should be and he's not sure how to cut it down. He's going to ask if they can run it in weekly installments.

When Landry went to Asheville High, and before she expanded her dating pool to college boys, I was constantly tapped as the resident expert on her favorite restaurants, bands, TV shows... It was fun to reprise my former role as consultant.

Paul made a gag-me face and left to work on his column, and I spent the rest of lunch helping Whit plan the perfect date. Unlike his predecessors, he seems to recognize that I'm a person in my own right. He'd read my last piece in the Chronicle and said something thoughtful about it. This is totally unexpected, but I could see us becoming friends.

Thursday, April 11th

Paul was mad because the entertainment editor wouldn't let him run his Fargo review in installments, and then he was mad at me because I told him I agreed with her.

Saturday, April 13th

Landry and Whit had their date tonight. I sat around drawing, keeping one eye on Whit's window. His light didn't turn on until 11:15, so I guess it went well.

Feeling unshiny, overlooked, and generally sorry for myself.

Wednesday, April 17th

Whit came over to study with Landry and me. He's in AP U.S. History, too, and she asked my permission before inviting him, so I was okay with it.

After history we worked on other stuff; I was polishing a piece for Honors English with the prompt, "Write a piece in the voice of Sylvia Plath." I usually freeze up when I try to write fiction—which we normally don't in this class—but I loved writing about what would've happened if, instead of killing herself, Sylvia kicked Ted Hughes to the curb and moved back to New York. She gets a makeover and a roommate, and on weekends she sends the kids to grandma's house and plays coffeehouses as a singer-songwriter. Whit read it and said it was "fun" and he loves my "voice."

I also found out that he thought Paul was my boyfriend since we always eat lunch together. Landry thought that was hilarious. She wants to set me up with Eric, who just got dumped by his girlfriend and thinks I'm cute. Supposedly.

I literally resolved to be noticed this year, but I feel so conflicted when it actually happens.

Thursday, April 18th

Landry gave Eric my number and he called me! We were on the phone for an hour! He's really easy to talk to and he laughed at my jokes and told me I'm cool. He said someone at his school is having a party on Saturday because their parents will be out of town, and a ton of people from both our schools will be there, so I should come, too. It's not really a date, but it's not NOT a date.

Friday, April 19th

Landry came over to tell me in person that Eric got back together with his ex. She was pissed on my behalf and felt guilty for being the one who got us together, but all I felt was vague annoyance. I knew he was too good-looking for me.

She still wants me to go to the party with her and Whit, but I begged off. Mom and Brandon and April are going out for pizza and a movie tomorrow and I guess I'm a loser 'cause that sounds like way more fun.

Saturday, April 20th

I felt a belated surge of regret about the party and asked Landry if it was too late to change my mind, and she was like, "Never!"

Mom was disappointed I was skipping the movie, but she gets why I want to go with Landry. After everyone left, I tried on every piece of clothing I own in a desperate, fruitless effort to find the razor-thin line between "don't care" and "trying way too hard."

I mixed things up and swapped my Black Honey for a glittery Jerome Russell gloss. I know glittery isn't the same thing as shiny, but it's close enough.

And now I'm waiting, waiting, waiting for the doorbell to ring.

They're late.

They're here!

Sunday, April 21st

~~I don't know how to~~

~~This is the worst~~

~~Last night~~

Fuck.

AAAAAA

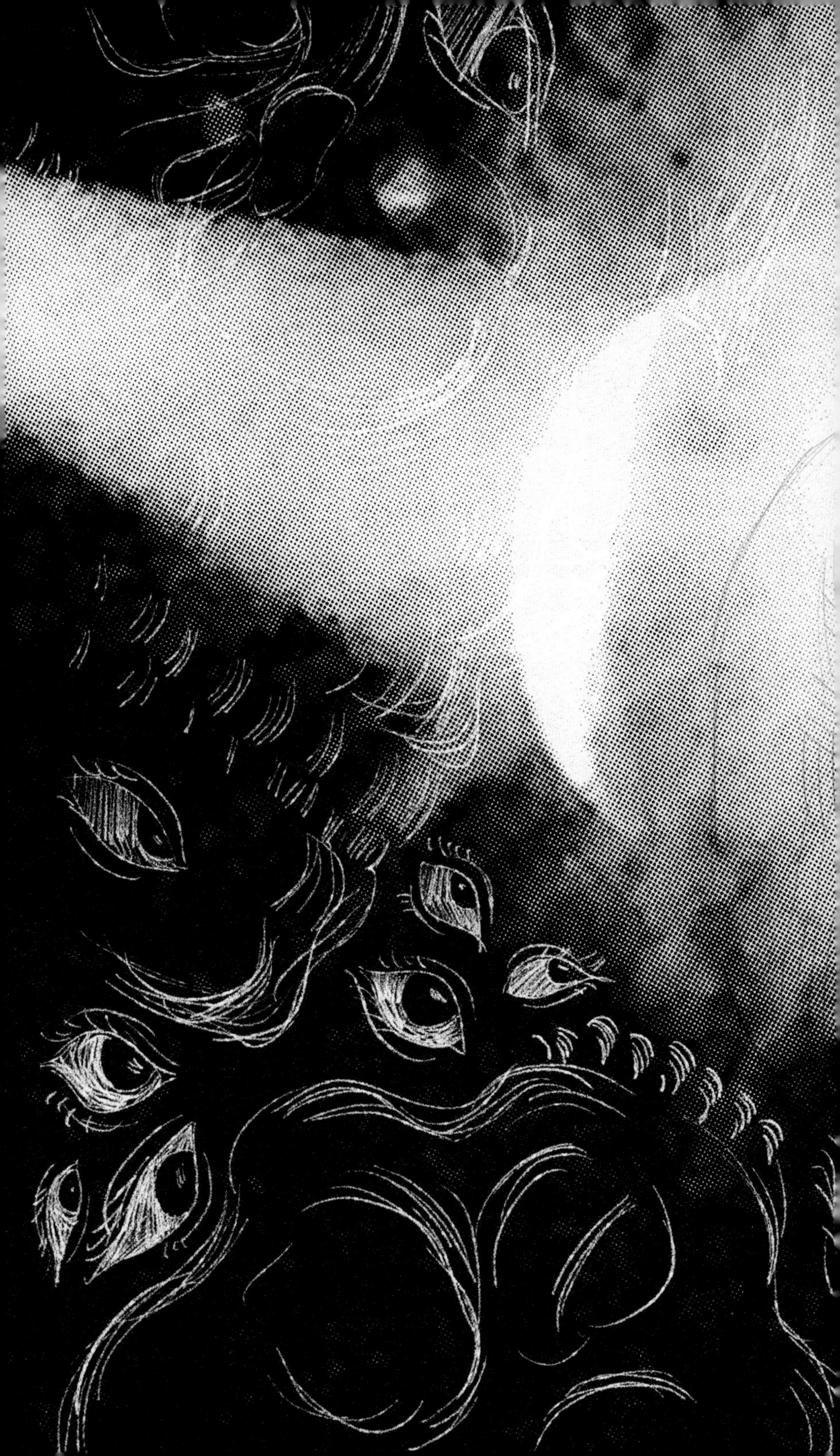

Tuesday, April 23rd

I know I should write about what happened, but I don't even want to think about it. I try to shut out the memories when I feel them surfacing, but at night, when everything's quiet and still, my subconscious pins me down, Clockwork Orange-style, and forces me to relive every awful moment.

Drawing is the only thing keeping me (somewhat) sane. When I'm drawing I can hide inside myself. Hide from myself. I slink away to a closet in the attic of my brain where it's dark and quiet and Saturday never happened.

Yesterday Paul ditched me at lunch; he wouldn't even look at me in English or at the Chronicle meeting. I cornered him in the hall and tried to apologize, but he told me to leave him alone and walked away. In history Whit shot me a pitying look, but he didn't try to talk to me.

Being shunned by Paul is a million times more painful than my breakup with Dave, a thousand times worse than me and Landry's friendship being over. I can see now that Landry and I have been sliding toward this moment for at least a year, and even though it sucks, part of me's grateful she said what she did. If she hadn't hurt me, I wouldn't have found the courage to get away from her.

But losing Paul? It sucks completely. I never imagined myself doing something so stupid, so completely unforgiveable. It doesn't feel anything but bad.

Saturday, April 27th

Mom took April and Brandon to dinner at Peking Garden. Not me, though. I'm still grounded.

It's been a week and I think I'm ready to get into it, so...

Here goes.

One Week Ago

Whit drove me and Landry to the party. It was at a house outside of town, with woods on all sides and no neighbors to call the cops. There was a bonfire, and everyone was standing around holding red Solo cups.

I spotted Kayla on the deck and split off from Landry and Whit to say hi and commiserate about the brutal week we've had in Trig. You know—normal, fun party small talk. She seemed happy to see me. She came with her boyfriend, but they had a fight in the car.

We're not going to, like, break up, but I can't be around him till I stop wanting to punch his dumb face.
Ugh. I get it.
See that guy by the keg? We were going to come together, but then he got back with his ex.
I bet that's her with him.
Gross, but I can top it.
The dude smoking on the deck? We made out in the prop room freshman year and he told everyone we had sex.
Everyone on Earth is at this party.
Right?
Even Paul and Jennifer are coming.

Excuse me?!
PAUL is coming to a party?

I know, right? I thought all he did was watch movies.
Yeah. And work on his screenplay.

He wrote a screenplay?

I thought Paul told everyone about Nuclear Submarine, but apparently not. Learning I was part of his inner circle made me feel kinda warm and special, a sensation enhanced by the beer we were drinking.

I usually don't let myself get drunk, but Landry was with a trustworthy guy, for once, and I knew Whit would drive us home, so I let my guard down. More and more people were showing up, including some goofy stoner dudes Kayla knew from school. We played hacky sack, which I suck at even when sober, but everyone else did, too. One of the dudes was kind of flirting with me, but before that could go anywhere, Landry came over and dragged me off to meet her friend Jon.

Looking back, if I'd just stood up for myself and told her no...but obviously, I didn't.

Jon was by the bonfire with Whit—they're friends, too, apparently—and the first thing he did was stick a camera in my face and take my picture. He was sitting down and I was standing, so he probably got a very artistic shot up my nose.

Then he told me I have "an air of sadness" in my face, but it's cool because "sad girls are sexy." I didn't know how to react to that, because I wasn't sad, and that's a weird thing to say to someone you just met, so I just stared at the fire.

He goes to Landry's school but thinks he'd fit in better at Asheville High, only his parents won't let him go there. I was like, hey, AHS is a good school—right, Whit? I figured he'd back me up, but he said it's just an "okay" school, and he only goes there because he's serious about his running and we have a great coach.

Jon's parents expect him to go to college next year and join the family business selling real estate, but he's planning to defer for a year and drive around in a VW bus taking photos of "the real America." I said that was cool and he invited me to come with him, because I seemed like I'd be "down for it."

What gave him the impression I'd be "down for" anything? Was it my sassy, glittery lips? My alluring air of sadness? Why would I want to go anywhere with someone I don't even know? Did he think I wouldn't be going to college, too?

Landry wasn't picking up on my "save me" looks, so I finally went to use the bathroom and just...didn't go back.

I got another beer and went over to the hacky sack dudes, who were sprawled on the grass, smoking pot and looking at the stars. I lay down next to them. Everything was spinning and I worried I'd fall off the Earth and vanish into the endlessly expanding universe. I closed my eyes and listened to them naming constellations: Orion. Cassiopeia. Sagittarius. Every few minutes, like a skipping record, the same guy pointed out Venus.

Someone handed me a joint, but I was already more fucked up than I'd planned to get, so I passed it on. The conversation turned to aliens and UFOs and jokes about being "probed." I don't know how much time passed, but all of a sudden Landry was there.

CRUNCH
CRUNCH
CRUNCH
What's wrong with you, Christine?
I have the spins.
No, why were you so rude to Jon?!
Um, he's creepy.
Creepy how?

I don't know. He just, like, skeeved me out.
He was trying to be NICE! God! I don't know why I bother.
So DON'T. I never asked you to fix my love life.
Oh, your love life? Try your WHOLE damn life!
You can't do anything without me holding your hand!

I fix your hair, your clothes...
and, like, before I smoothed things over, you and Whit didn't talk for YEARS!
If it wasn't for me, you wouldn't even be at this party!
If it wasn't for ME you'd still be lost downtown after your shithead ex dumped you curbside!

You're mean when you drink.
I was just LYING here! Maybe if you left me alone instead of HASSLING me–

All I do is stick my neck out for you and you're such an ungrateful bitch!
Ever since your dad died you've had this whole VICTIM complex and I'm SICK of it!

NEXT THING I KNEW, I WAS PUSHING HER DOWN.

Huh?!
HEY!

LET ME GO!

CHRISTINE! It's me!

Paul?

Come on. Let's get you some air.

He took me to the edge of the woods and we sat on a log. I didn't throw up, just dry-heaved and cried a lot. I'd never been in a fight before—not a physical one. I told him what Landry said to me, and even though he's a pacifist he agrees that she crossed the line.

I didn't know how badly I needed to hear that. It was the nicest thing anyone ever said to me.

SO I KISSED HIM.

It just seemed like the thing to do.

He kissed me back.

Maybe it was reflexive.

Maybe I caught him off guard.

But it wasn't a one-sided thing.

I shouldn't have done that.

You can't tell Jennifer.

I won't. I'm sorry.

She's always been paranoid that—
I told her we're just friends.

I don't even like you like that, Paul. I don't know why I—

I just—
I—
I'm drunk.

Wow. Fuck you.

I called a cab from the house. When I got home, Mom instantly knew I was drunk and put me to bed with ibuprofen and Gatorade, just like she does when I'm sick. She barely lectured me—her whole thing is, "You can't grow up if you don't mess up"—but I'm grounded for a month. No TV, car, friends. (What friends?)

I fell asleep with two images looping in my head:

If I'm honest, I don't regret fighting Landry, but I wish to God I hadn't kissed Paul.

He won't even look at me anymore.

Saturday, May 18th

I haven't written in a while. I haven't even wanted to draw. I feel totally empty.

Landry and I still aren't speaking, and I doubt we ever will again. Whit and I have gone back to not speaking. Paul won't talk to me, even at Chronicle meetings. Sometimes I eat lunch with Kayla (she's sorry about what happened at the party and didn't want to take sides) or Peace, but mostly I'm keeping to myself. The school year's almost over so there's no better time to be a pariah.

As of today I'm not grounded anymore, but I feel very, like, whatever about regaining my freedom. I celebrated by driving Brandon and April to Biltmore Square—the OTHER mall. I didn't want to risk running into Landry. Mom gave April permission to get her ears pierced, but when we got to Claire's she chickened out. I get it—they put the piercing chair in the window and everyone walking by can watch you get punched full of holes. I wanted to show her it's not so bad, so I got my ears double-pierced, which I've always wanted to do. That convinced her to go for it. She held my hand so tight and I felt like the world's best big sister.

When we came out, we found Brandon standing outside Frederick's of Hollywood, drooling over the headless plastic mannequins in trashy lingerie. He pretended he hadn't been, so April and I teased him all the way to the food court.

When we got there, we ran into a pack of girls from his class, and they were all giggling and kicking each other under the table. I was like, damn, Brandon's hot shit for a seventh grader! How did he go from kicking trees in the park to class stud in, like, a month?

When Landry and I were Brandon's age, little clusters of middle school boys would follow us around the mall and find excuses to talk to Landry. Even then I knew they didn't care about me; I just happened to be there.

Monday, May 20th

The academic awards were tonight. I got a journalism award for my article, "The Problem with Prom," and ended up on stage next to Paul, who got one for creative writing. Awkward. JennIFER was in the audience, looking proud. I wonder what he told her about why he's not friends with me anymore.

Mom's over the moon about the award. She's acting like that alone will get me a full ride to the college of my choice. On the way home, while I was (privately) moping about missing Paul, Mom was fretting about how much she'll miss me when I leave for school. My first choice is UNC-Chapel Hill, which is six hours away, but she thinks I should go to UNC-Asheville and live at home to save on rent. It makes financial sense, but the thought of staying in town makes me feel like I've been buried alive.

The more I think about it, the more I'm afraid that the only way I'll ever be shiny is if I get out of Asheville and go to a place where no one knows me and start over.

I didn't say any of that to Mom, of course. I just told her I'd think about it.

Wednesday, May 22nd

Brandon is taking Claire, one of the girls from the mall, to the movies on Saturday. Mom offered to buy my ticket if I'd chaperone. I think she was hoping an outing would cheer me up. She doesn't know the details of what happened with me and Landry, but it's kind of obvious we're not talking.

Friday, May 24th

Kayla and I went to Beanstreets to prep for our Trig final and ran into Peace, who just found out he got accepted to the NC School of the Arts for senior year. He's moving to Winston-Salem this summer.

I told him I'm happy for him, which is true, but I'm also WILDLY jealous because how DARE he escape from this hellhole and leave me here? I'll still have Kayla, but she's going to work as a counselor at some camp where she's been going since she was a kid, so I'm staring down the barrel of a long, lonely, boring-ass summer.

But there's hope! When I went to VideoLife to rent movies for me and the kiddies:

Can I please have an application?
That depends.
On?
What you're renting.

Ohhhhh.

Hm. The new Mary-Kate and Ashley Olsen teenybopper vehicle.

My little brother has a crush on them!

And...gritty thriller Se7en.

They balance each other out, right?

No worries. The application process includes a thorough review of your rental history.
heh heh
BE KIND REWIND

I think he was joking, but maybe not?! The application asks you to name your favorite movie and I spent ages trying to figure out what I could pick that would make them hire me. Chinatown? Rear Window? Pulp Fiction? I took a leap of faith and wrote down my actual favorite movie, which is The Princess Bride.

I probably won't get the job, but oh my God, I WANT it! As far as jobs I can walk to, it's VideoLife or Peking Garden across the street.

I know Mom expects me to watch Brandon and April all summer, but a girl can dream.

Sunday, May 26th

Brandon and Claire are now officially "going out," which is surprising since I detected no romance between them at the movies last night. Maybe it was because I was preoccupied by seeing Whit and Landry in front of us in the ticket line. It felt like seeing a ghost, but they didn't notice me, so maybe I was the ghost, not them.

Wednesday, May 29th

I got the job. I GOT THE JOB!!! They loved my favorite movie pick! I start next week! Reduced hours at first, then more once school's out.

I made my case to Mom, fully expecting her to make me turn it down, but she said it's okay! Brandon and April are old enough to stay home alone and she'll arrange rides to their summer activities. I'll still need to help with meals and stuff, but holy crap, this is happening! First VideoLife, then college, then Sassy, then the world! And maybe, if I save enough money, I can really buy a car.

Monday, June 3rd

It's finals week. Everyone's got their heads down and their blinders on. I go to school, I take exams, I study...and I'm officially a VideoLife employee. ☺

The guy who trained me, Jamal, was the same guy who was teasing me the day I applied. He did two semesters at UNC-A, decided it was bullshit, and dropped out. He wants to be a cinematographer, but for now he spends a lot of time walking around town with a video camera, shooting random stuff. He knows a lot about movies and he's always trying to stump me on trivia like character actors' names. He thinks I have very "mainstream" taste and need to "expand my palate."

That's the kind of thing Paul would say. I wish I could introduce them. I wish I could tell Paul I'm working here.

Thursday, June 6th

The first person I knew who came into the store during my first real shift today was Whit. He'd walked down with Reggie to return Before Sunrise and I was like, "Surprise! I work here now." He actually seemed happy to see me. I asked how he liked the movie, which is like the most romantic film ever, but he was bringing it back for his parents. I said he should watch it with Landry and he told me they broke up right after I saw them at the movies.

She's a bitch and she doesn't deserve my sympathy, but I hope she's doing okay.

Friday, June 7th

The school year is basically over. I handed in my last paper and picked up my yearbook. My picture feels like an artifact from a parallel dimension. That version of me had a boyfriend and TWO best friends. I want to smack the idiot smile off her face.

When I got off the school bus and walked up the alley, Whit was coming through the gate with Reggie, who got loose and jumped all over me. Whit ran after him, apologizing. Reggie'd been inside all day so he was extra wound up. I said it was fine; I feel like that, too, now that school's almost out

I made an effort not to grill him about Landry, but he'd clearly been dying to rehash the breakup. Apparently she dumped him because they weren't "clicking," which I know means she thinks he's boring.

Whit says she was upset about our fight for a while—he's the one who pulled her off me—and she felt awful about the things she said, and especially about bringing my dad into it. Which made me feel a lot of ways. I was almost tempted to call her and make nice and put things back the way they were, but the longer we go without talking, the more I realize I don't miss her or her drama.

I didn't want to keep talking about Landry, so I changed the subject. Whit and I really do have a lot in common. We both want to move to New York and see what it's like to live in a place where things actually happen, and we both love to read—although I think he was disappointed when I admitted that, aside from books I read for school, I mostly read magazines.

He said he's in a Vonnegut phase—he's going to loan me Cat's Cradle when he's finished it—and his favorite book is On the Road. Kerouac wrote it in three weeks, and Whit thinks that's how you write "fresh" prose—you sit down and spew out a few hundred pages without thinking too much about it beforehand. His goal is to have a novel published by the time he's twenty-one, and next summer he's planning to shut himself up in a room and go on a "writing bender." He'd do it this year, but he and his parents are spending a big chunk of the summer visiting relatives in Texas and he "can't write there." No idea why not, but to each their own.

Monday, June 10th

It's the last day of school. JennIFER and Paul passed me outside the cafeteria and refused to make eye contact. So long, jerks. See you in August.

I think I'm going to grow my hair out this summer. I've never had hair past my shoulders, and who knows, maybe I'd like being a long-haired girly-girl. I don't even need to dye it back to my natural color, 'cause the red and purple bits have faded enough that the roots aren't obvious.

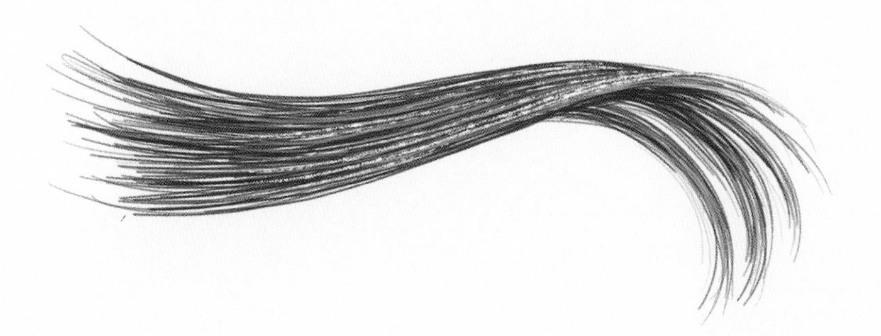

Friday, June 14th

I ran into Whit when I was leaving work and we had another spontaneous hang. I told him about today's memorable customers: this lady we call Cry for Help, who comes in every Friday to rent incredibly sad movies, and the creep who gives us multipage lists of Japanimation he expects us to order.

Right now Whit's parents are throwing an evening pool party and I'm spying on it from my room. They have catered food and a DJ, and the pool's glowing a glorious mood-ring aquamarine, but no one's swimming. What's the point of a pool party if you won't get in the water?! I would, in a heartbeat.

Saturday, June 15th

Whit said the party was boring. It was all his parents' friends talking to him about his capital-F Future. I was like, "Did they tell you to get into plastics?" He didn't catch the reference to The Graduate, but it's okay; I already knew he isn't into movies.

I almost suggested we watch it together, but that would be kind of intimate and we're just friends.

Sunday, June 16th

It was a million degrees today and I sweated out half my body weight on the walk home from work, so naturally that was the moment Whit chose to open his gate and invite me in.

His parents were out, driving Reggie to some posh dog boarding place an hour away, so we dangled our legs in the pool and drank Coronas. He even cut slices of lime like in the commercials. The whole thing felt unreal—the heat, the cicadas, the alcohol. He'd been swimming and microscopic drops of water were clinging to his chest hair. I made myself focus on the cold bottle pressed against my leg and the dead moth floating by, and not how close we were sitting.

Tomorrow he'll fly to Dallas, and when he comes back he'll probably never speak to me again.

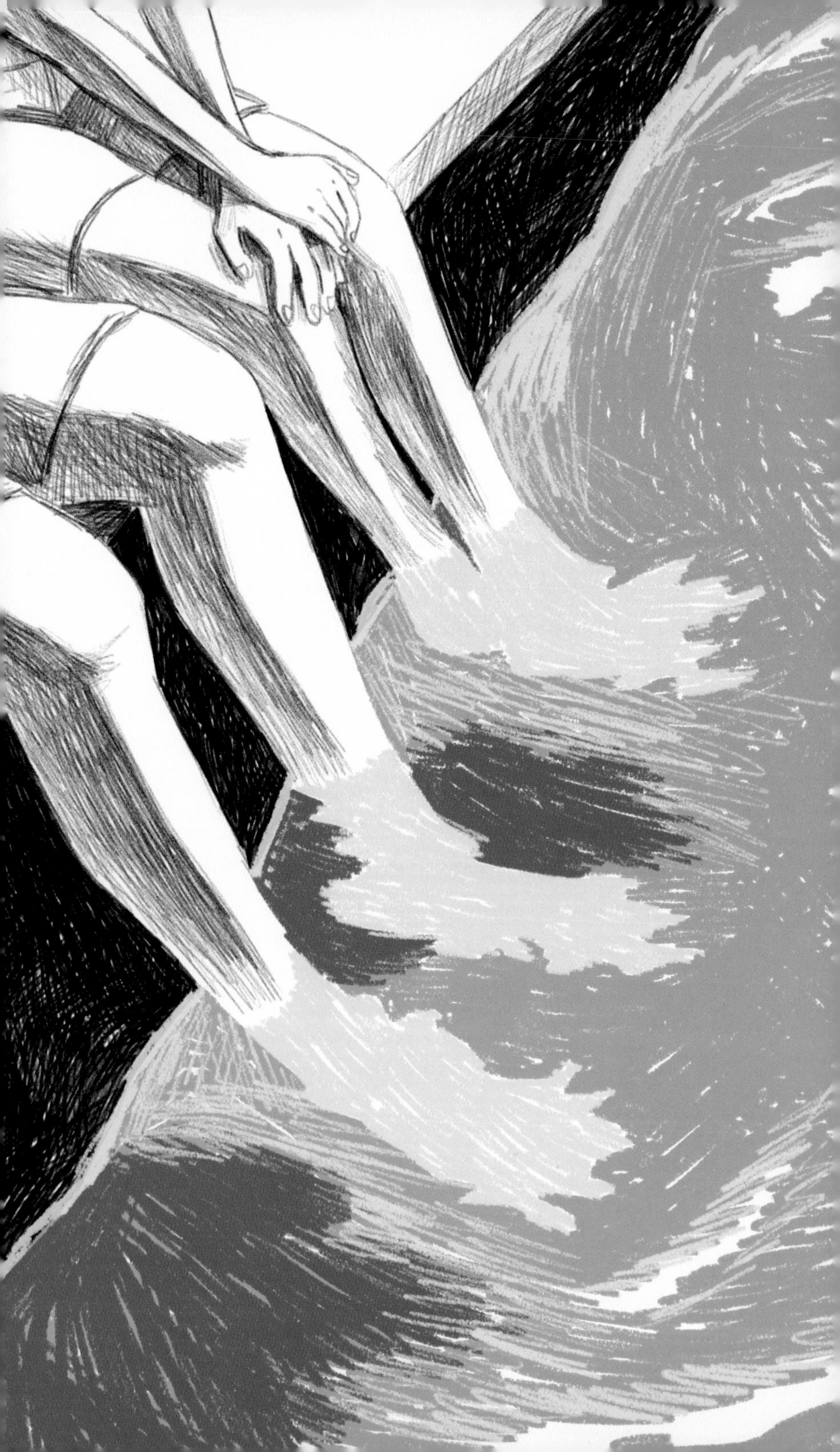

Monday, June 17th

When I got up this morning I found Whit's copy of <u>Cat's Cradle</u> at the back door. Inside was a note.

5:30 a.m.

En route to airport. As promised, here's the book. Give it a chance; I think you'll *get* something out of it. I'm also including my grandparents' address. Let's write each other letters like they did back in the day. Let's tell each other secrets.

Yours in Bokononism (you'll *get* that once you've read the book),

Whit

Thursday, June 20th

"Let's tell each other secrets."

Every time I reread that line, the hairs on the back of my neck stand up. He's flirting with me, right? Or testing me. Is there something specific he wants to find out? This is like long-distance Truth or Dare.

I started my reply the day he left and went through multiple drafts, but I didn't mail it until today. Didn't want to seem desperate.

I thanked him for lending me Cat's Cradle, which is one of the weirdest books I've read. Was Vonnegut on drugs when he wrote it, or does it just seem that way? I heard Kerouac wrote On the Road on speed, so I'm getting the impression that all of Whit's favorite books were written by people under the influence.

I told him my favorite book is Jane Eyre, but now that I think about it, I don't like the part where she's at school and her friend dies of consumption, or the part where she gets romantically entangled with the creepy minister dude, and I go back and forth on whether or not I like the ending. But the part where she's falling in love with Mr. Rochester and solving the mystery of the mad woman in the house—that part is perfection. It makes up for the rest.

I said I relate to Jane because I feel like an outsider in my own life. There aren't many people who know the real me, especially now that Landry and I aren't friends. I have this fear that if I show anyone the weird/dark/sad parts of me, I'll scare them away. I hope I don't scare him away, too, but he wouldn't be the first.

That set the stage for my secret, chosen after long deliberation. The summer after fifth grade, my family went on a cruise. There was a boy my age in the next cabin. Adam. He and I ran around together for a week, and by the end I was completely infatuated with him. We never kissed or held hands or anything, but we exchanged addresses, and when I got home I wrote him a letter professing my love. I even cut out little paper hearts and put them in the envelope. He never wrote me back. And that was the last time I wrote a letter to a boy.

Saturday, June 22nd

I did something crazy tonight. I went swimming in Whit's pool.

Mom was at work and I wasn't, and TV had claimed April and Brandon. I went out in the backyard to watch fireflies, and I could hear the pool filter gurgling over the fence. On impulse I tried his gate. It was unlocked, so I went in.

I swam in my underwear. I'm not an exhibitionist or an adrenaline junkie, so it was a big deal for me, even though there was no chance I'd get caught. It felt amazing to trespass, to be bad, and for a second I thought how proud Landry would be of me. It's just like the kind of stupid shit she does.

I sneaked back into the house so Brandon and April wouldn't catch me dripping wet and almost wiped out on the hardwood floor.

Before I went to bed I got the photo albums down and looked for old pictures of me and Whit. For a few years he's there at my birthday parties with Landry and a lot of other kids, and then he disappears. And then the photos stop, because Dad wasn't there to take them anymore.

Wednesday, June 26th

6/23/96

Christine,

Texas is hot as balls. I went running and it felt like being cooked on a giant griddle. This is not a place where humans were meant to live. In more ways than one it's like visitng another planet.

My grandparents live in Highland Park, which is the richest town in Texas. All the houses are mansions with full-time maids and threatening signs that say "Armed Guard On Premises". In comparison, our neighborhood looks like a trailer park. My cousin Haven just turned 16 and got a new Beemer. When my mom turned 16, she got a new nose. Sometimes I wonder who I'd be if I'd grown up here, too.

I know what you mean, feeling like an outsider in your life—especially when I'm in Texas, but at home, too. My parents think I'm a good boy who'll grow into the person they expect me to be, and my friends—they're just people I'm killing time with until I get out of Asheville.

Have you heard of MK-Ultra? Sometimes I think I've been brainwashed and I'm a secret agent waiting to be activated by a code word. Then everything will make sense.

Yes, most of my favorite authors were on drugs and/or insane. I like books that look at the world from a fresh perspective. I don't see the point of books where you can tell from page one how they're going to end. I want to write a novel that dispenses with all the ordinary plots and stock characters and breaks new ground. I might even drop acid before I start my novel. I hear it opens your mind up to new possibilities.

I assume you finished Cat's Cradle. What did you think? Jane Eyre isn't my bag, but I'm going to check it out. I think it'll help me to understand you better—'cause I want to. It sucks I had to leave just when we were starting to get to know each other. Don't worry; you can't scare me off by being weird and dark. I thrive on that shit.

That boy who didn't write you back was a moron. So, am I the first guy to write you a letter? I like that.

Oh yeah—I owe you a secret. Here goes: Remember when my friend Jon took your photo at that party? I made him print me a copy. I brought it to Texas and I'm looking at it right now.

Whit

Oh my God. He really does like me.

He says I can't scare him away.

He likes being the first guy to write me a letter.

He's looking at a picture of me.

That party was ages ago, in a past life. So when did Whit ask for the picture? Was it when he was still with Landry? Was he thinking about me even then? Wondering if I'd be a better girlfriend? There's no way. But is there?

I wrote Whit back and kept it light. I said I noticed Jon taking that picture, and it was for sure a weird angle—like, straight up my nose. Are my nostrils cute? Do they have an attractive shape? Is Whit into nostrils? Because, ew!

Then I changed the subject to how, when I was walking to work today, I saw someone rob the Exxon across the street—in broad daylight, too. Jamal said it's not the first time he's seen them get held up. I said I don't get how people end up robbing gas stations and living a life of crime, and he just rolled his eyes and said, "Of course you don't."

It bugged me all day. Like, yeah, I'm naive, but I'm not a total innocent. To prove it to myself, after work (and I obviously didn't put this part in my letter) I swam in Whit's pool again. I wore a suit this time, and while I was in the water, I imagined how it would feel to kiss Whit.

I have a confession.
When you were in Texas, I swam in your pool.
I know.

What?! How?

I can't explain how, but I could, like, sense that you'd been here.

When I got in the water it was like you were there with me.
Your body pressed up against my body.
Like this?

Afterward I went up to the house and peeked in the ground-floor windows. The blinds weren't pulled all the way down so I could see into the kitchen. It was big and spotless, except for one lonely coffee mug sitting on the counter. Waiting for the boy who lives there to come back home.

Later, I suddenly remembered the one time I did something "bad." When I was ten, I was at the library and I wanted to read this bodice-ripper romance with Fabio on the cover, but I was too embarrassed to check it out, so I stole it. I did eventually return it to the drop box, so in the end, does that count as theft? It's funny now, but at the time I was so ashamed that I didn't tell anyone—not even Landry.

I added the story to my letter. I hope it makes Whit laugh. I hope he sends me another secret, too.

Tuesday, July 2nd

6/29/96

Christine,

My cousin Scott, Haven's older brother, comes home every summer to go camping, which means going to a hunting ranch in the middle of nowhere with his guy friends and getting obliterated. This was the first year I was invited, and I was surprised my parents let me go, but then again, my dad seems relieved whenever I show signs of becoming a red-blooded American male.

It was exactly what you'd expect. We drank and played poker and shot guns at beer cans. Scott rambled endlessly about his frat initiation and all the girls he's banged at school. I used to look up to him, but now I can see he's an idiot. I never want to be a guy like that.

At one point I went to the woods to pee and this beautiful buck walked out of the trees, and I thought how sad it was that he was destined to be killed for sport by some rich dude and mounted on a wall. I wish you could've seen it.

I've been thinking about you a lot, and I'm sorry it took the whole thing with Landry for us to be friends. And I'm sorry I wasn't there for you when your dad died. At the time I didn't know what to say, but that's no excuse. Forgive me?

I'm looking at your photo again, and don't worry, your nostrils look great.

Whit

P.S.
Cute secret. Here's one from me: the first time I got turned on was watching Babs Bunny on Tiny Toons. I owe my sexual awakening to a pink cartoon rabbit.

It meant a lot to hear Whit apologize. It wasn't all in my head, the way he and his family shut us out. And this thing between us—it's not in my head, either.

I told him I forgive him. That I've been thinking about him, too. That I wish I could have seen the deer.

That I finished Cat's Cradle and kind of hated it. Sorry? It's brilliant but too, like, nihilistic. Why are important books always so bleak? I don't need a book to tell me nothing happens for a reason; I learned that when my dad died. Fate and magic and the afterlife are just things humans made up to feel better.

(Is that too dark, Whit? Were you telling the truth when you said I wouldn't scare you away? I really hope you were.)

To lighten things up, I wrote about how much I love my job. My coworkers are awesome, especially Jamal. He's cool. He worked as a PA on some of the movies that filmed here, and next summer he's moving to Los Angeles. I think he's going to make it out there; he showed me this tape he made of a band playing in one of the old buildings downtown, and it looked like something that could be on MTV.

Uh-oh, now I'm feeling gloomy again. How does everyone else know where they'll be a year from now?! Jamal's going to LA. Whit's writing his novel before he heads off to Yale. Me? No clue. I'll be leaving for college, but which one? UNC–Chapel Hill, hopefully. It has a great student paper.

Then I was like, "Hey, speaking of the future, when are you coming home?"

Wednesday, July 3rd

Whit's pool isn't the only place I've been sneaking around; I've been snooping through Paul's rental history, too. I haven't run into him at work yet—he's managed to only come by when I'm not on the schedule—but he's been in multiple times. He's on a whole French New Wave kick.

Then I thought I might as well check and see what Whit's rented, too, and I almost wish I hadn't. For a guy with a hard-on for capital-L Literature, he has horrific taste in movies. I know he shares an account with his parents, but I doubt they're the ones who've repeatedly rented *Road House* and *Ace Ventura: Pet Detective*. We all contain multitudes, or whatever.

In the interest of fairness, I pulled up my family's account, because what if it was just as bad as Whit's? And no, it's not an impeccable record of taste and refinement, but I share it with Brandon and April, and Mom, so that's not entirely my fault. As I went deeper into our rental history, it started to get weird. First, there were the movies Landry and I picked together, then there were movies I'd rented with Dad, and things he'd rented with Mom, and it was almost too much to take. I felt like I was reading my life story, one VHS at a time.

Maybe the point of movies is more than entertainment or intellectual stimulation, it's so we can remember where and when and who we were the first time we watched *Casablanca*. Or *Singing in the Rain*. Or *The Last Unicorn*.

Or even *Ace Ventura: Pet Detective*.

Thursday, July 4th

Mom, Brandon, April, and I walked down to the golf course to sit on the green and watch the Grove Park Inn's fireworks display. The last time I was here I was with Landry, and she was here this time, too; I was expecting to see her since pretty much the whole neighborhood turns out on Independence Day. She was sitting with her dad, but her mom was MIA. Mom volunteered that she heard Landry's parents are having a trial separation and maybe Landry would like it if I reached out to her.

I couldn't be like, "Actually, Mom, Landry and I had a fight—we came to blows and everything—and now I'm embroiled in an epistolary flirtation with her ex-boyfriend."

So I just said, "I doubt that very much."

Friday, July 5th

Kayla sent me a short note from camp, but still no letter from Whit. I thought I'd get one by now, but now that I think about it, the last one I sent him was a lot to process.

Today, when I looked in Whit's kitchen window after swimming, the lonely mug was gone! It hadn't occurred to me that they'd still have a maid come clean their empty house, but I guess that's the kind of thing you do when money is no object. Then I heard the clink of the gate and for a second wondered if it was Whit and his parents coming home. But it was just the pool guy.

I abandoned my towel on the lounge chair and sprinted around the side of the house and out the front. I had to walk all the way around the block in bare feet and a wet bathing suit.

In retrospect, I could've gotten away with it if I wasn't such a dork. I could've told the guy I had permission to swim, and would he even care if I didn't? A truly shiny person, like Landry, would act like they had every right to be there. That's the essence of shiny-ness, really: simultaneously standing out and looking like you belong.

I'll go back tomorrow for the towel, but after that, my life as a trespasser is over.

Monday, July 8th

Still no letter from Whit. Fuck. Is he mad 'cause I said I hated Cat's Cradle? Did I scare him away?

I chaperoned Brandon to his ice cream date with Claire, and Claire's big sister, Ashley, came, too. She runs cross-country so I asked, casually, if she knew "my neighbor Whit." She told me a whole story about how she and Whit "kind of" had a thing together. They never officially dated, but they were running buddies, and there was "definitely" something between them—until she asked him on a real date, and he said no, and things got super awkward.

It feels like there's something between me and Whit, too, but what if I'm just his letter buddy? What if he sensed things going too far and backed off, and that's why he hasn't written? Was I stupid to think he ever saw me as anything but a friend?!

Thursday, July 11th

7/9/96

Christine,

I keep trying to write you but there's too much I want to say. I'd rather do it in person.

I get back on the 15th.

Only six more days.

I'm saving my last secret till then.

Whit

OH MY GOD.

HE'S COMING HOME ON MY BIRTHDAY.

I got all in my head after hearing Ashley's story, but this is a totally different situation.

"Only six more days." He's counting the days till he sees me. Until he can tell me, in person, the secret he won't put in a letter. He doesn't have to write more than thirty-seven words because he knows he'll see me in less than a week.

Friday, July 12th

In three days.

Saturday, July 13th

In two days.

Sunday, July 14th

Tomorrow.

The only thought in my head is his name, rattling around my skull like a marble in a Mason jar. I stare at his yearbook photo and think, Whit's coming home tomorrow.

Whit. Home. Tomorrow.

Whit. Home. Whit. Tomorrow.

Whit. Whit. Whit. Whit. Whit.

Whit
Whit Whit Whit Whit Whit
Whit Whit Whit
Whit Whit Whit Whit
Whit Whit Whit Whit Whit
Whit Whit Whit Whit Whit
Whit Whit Whit Whit Whit
Whit Whit Whit Whit Whit
Whit Whit Whit Whit Whit

Whit

Whit Wh

Whit

Whit

Whit

Whit

Whit Whit Wh

Whit

Whit Whit W

Whit Wh Whit

Whi

Whit Whit

Whit Whit Whit Whit

Whit Whit

Whit Whit Whit Whit Whit

Whit Whit Whit Wh

Whit Whit

Whit Whit Whit Whit Whit

Whit Whit Whit Whit

hit Whit Whit Whit Whit Whit

Whit Whit

Whit Whit Whit Whit Whi

Whit Whit

Whit Whit Whit Whit Whit

Whit Whit Whit Whit Whit

Whit Whit Whit Whit Whit Whit Whit

hit Whit Whit Whit

Whit Whit

Whit

Whit Whit

Wh

Whit

Whit Wh

Whit

Whit Wh

Whit Whit

Whit

Whit

Whit Whit

Whit Whit Whit

Whit Whit Whit

Whit Wh Whit Whit

Whit Whit Whit

Whit Whit Whit

Whit Whit Whit Whit

Whit Whit Whit Whit

Whit Whit Whit

Whit Whit Whit

Whit Whit Whit

Whit Whit Whit

Whit Whit Whit

Whit Whit

Whit

Whit Whit

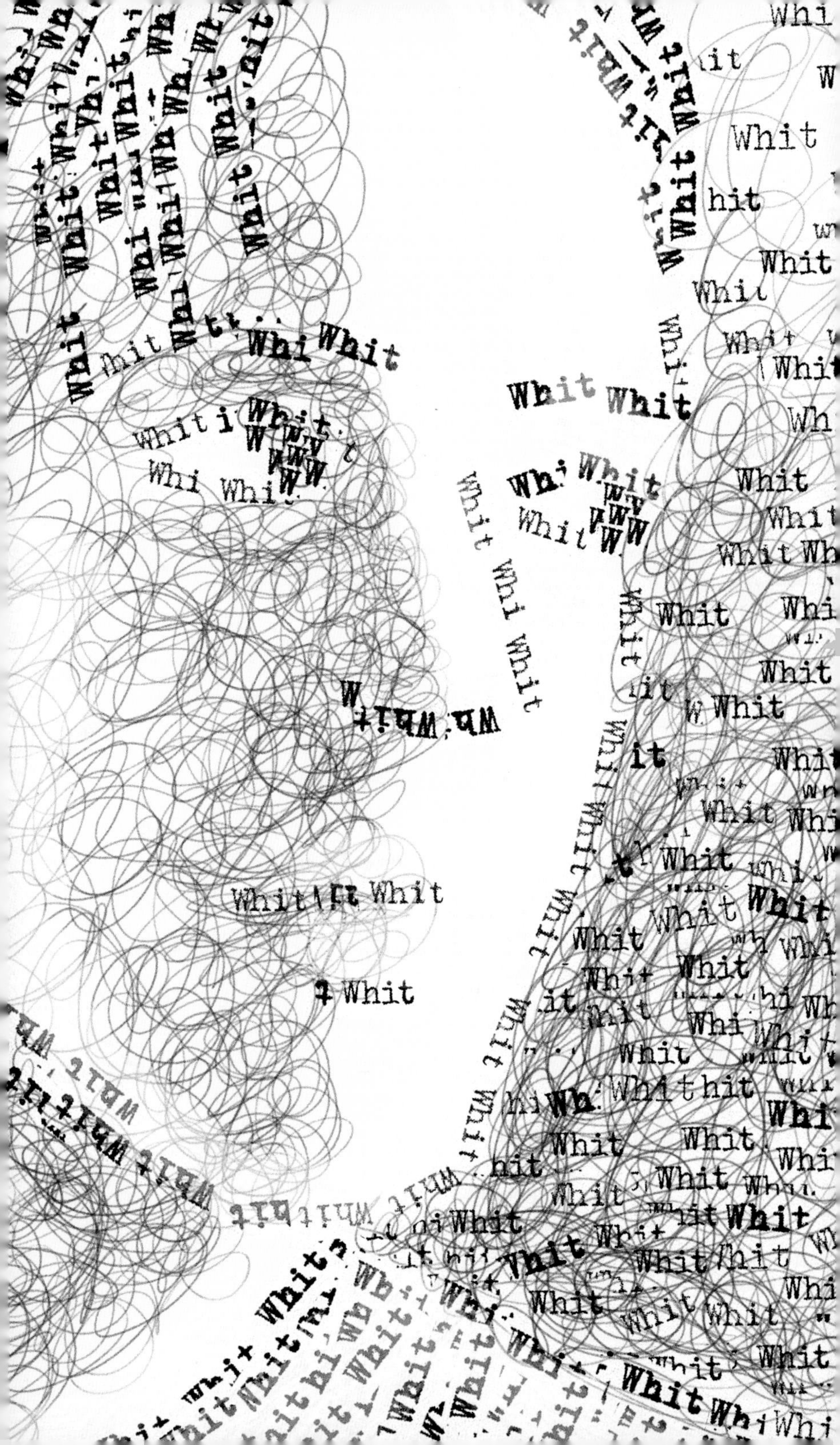

Whit

Whit

Whit

hit

Whit

Whit

Whit

Whit Whi Whit

Whit Whit

Whit Whit

Whit i Whit

Whi Whit

Whi Whit

Whit

Whit Wh

Whit

Whit

Whit

Whit

Whit Whit

Whit

Whit Whit

Whit

Whit

Whit Whit

Whit Whit

Whit

Whit Whit

Whit

Whit Whit

Whit

Whit Whit

Whit Whit

Whit Whit

Whit Whit

Whit Whit

Whit

Monday, July 15th

I'm seventeen today and my coworkers bought me a sheet cake from Ingles.

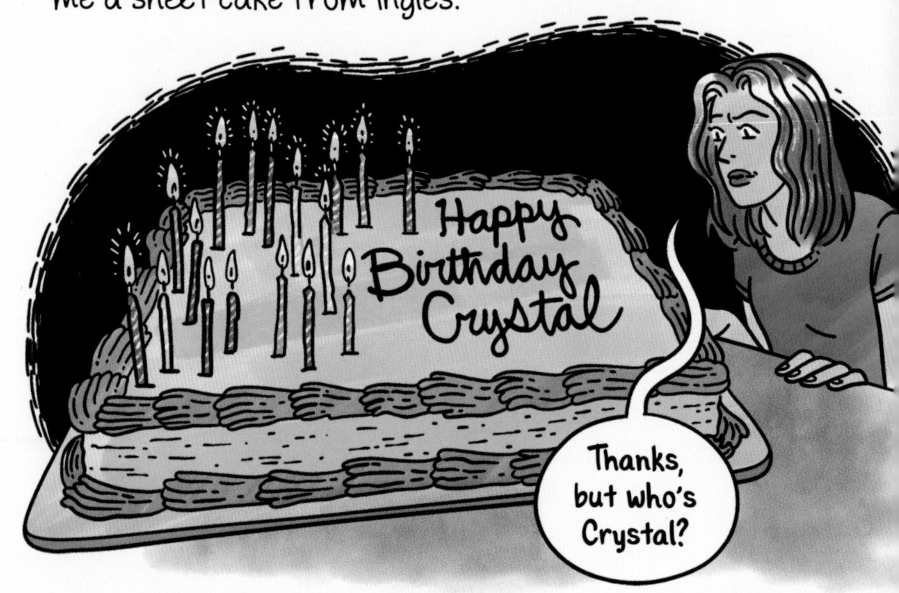

Jamal didn't notice the cake person got my name wrong until he got it back to the store. He felt shitty, but I think it's hilarious, and now everyone's calling me Crystal. My first inside-joke nickname!

Suzanne, one of the regulars, offered to read my palm. She does professional psychic readings at the Goddess Store and she said the next year will take me far from home. Hopefully that means I'll go to school somewhere other than UNC-A, but it could also mean that I'm embarking on a spiritual journey, not a physical one. Either way, it will take me closer to where I'm meant to be.

She also said she can sense that I have a "powerful spirit." Uh, sure.

Mom, April, and Brandon gave me tiny white gold hoops and star-shaped studs, which I can wear now that my new ear piercings are all healed up, and a bag of fun-size Snickers and a Funfetti cake. I ate too many pink icing roses and felt nauseous because according to Mom, the essence of seventeen is "old enough to know better but not old enough to do better." I hope I never grow up enough to decline an icing rose.

Part of me was holding my breath, waiting for Landry to call or swing by with a present. She always gave the best ones, not because they were expensive, but because they reminded me that she was paying attention. We'd be at the mall and I'd mention how I loved a sweater or a poster, and months later, when I'd forgotten I'd ever wanted it, she'd hand it to me in a gift bag with three colors of tissue paper sticking out the top. I wonder if there's a gift stuffed in the back of her closet—something she bought for me and set aside before the shit went down. Guess I'll never know.

But anyway, I got everything I wanted—except for seeing Whit. I know he's back. The car's in the driveway. The light's on in his room. He's probably busy unpacking. Decompressing. But part of me hoped he'd rush over to sweep me off my feet.

Tuesday, July 16th

Good! My birthday was yesterday, so everyone's been nice to me.

Shit! I've gotta get you something.
Nah.

Come on. What do you want?
YOU.
Um... nothing.

I have an idea, but I'm not sure you'll like it.

Give me a hint.

A hint.
Okay...

Follow me!

Um, Whit?
This part of the park's full of poison ivy.

That's why it's perfect. We're definitely all alone.

You know when you hear a song on the radio and it's, like, the best song you ever heard, but you don't know what it's called, and you're constantly hoping you'll hear it again so you can find out?
The whole time I was gone, that's how I felt about you.
That's my secret, Christine.

You were the song I wanted to hear.

Happy birthday.

Wednesday, July 17th

Kissing with Whit is nice. His kisses are damp but not sloppy. On a scale of dead-fish-tongue Dave to forbidden drunken kiss with Paul, he's somewhere in between.

Today, before I left for my shift, we made out at his house. Both his parents work, so no one's home during the day—except Fridays when their cleaner comes. His room is the masculine version of Landry's, with a dark maroon color palette instead of pastels, and bold stripes instead of delicate flowers. Everything matches: the curtains, the bedspread, the freaking wastebasket. Are any rich kids allowed to decorate their own rooms?

The only part that looked like he had a say in it was the bookshelf. On the top shelf are glass boxes of running medals and trophies, and all the other shelves are filled with his books: Burroughs, Ginsberg, Kerouac, Salinger, the collected Shakespeare. He also has one of those huge dictionaries that comes with a magnifying glass.

Kissing aside, the best part of being there was seeing Jane Eyre on his nightstand with a bookmark halfway through. He's really reading it! People always say they'll read the book or watch the movie you suggest, but they never mean it. He did.

I smiled at him and flipped it open to see what part he was at and realized the bookmark was a photo of a girl. For a second I felt sick. Who is she, and why does Whit have her photo?! Then I realized the girl was me. It's an arty, black-and-white shot of my face, and it's not as nostril-forward as I was afraid it would be. I'm half in darkness, half in firelight, and I look mysterious. And (Jon was right) a little sad. And surprisingly pretty.

Whit was watching my reaction and my face must have done something weird 'cause he asked if I was okay. I said yeah, but I wish the photo was less good. Is it disappointing to see me in real life, without perfect lighting and all that? He laughed and told me I'm ridiculous and kissed me again.

Saturday, July 20th

Sunday, July 21st

It's disgusting how into Whit I am. I never felt like this with Dave. I go around all day drunk on Whit's hair, lips, eyes, skin. I didn't know it was possible to be so infatuated you're, like, high. I'm using a gallon of foundation a day to cover the makeout burn from his stubble.

I can't comprehend why Landry let him go. But maybe it didn't feel like this for her. She's much more experienced than I am, so maybe she's built up a tolerance and I'm still a total lightweight. Maybe they didn't have the chemistry we do.

I haven't told Mom (or, duh, Brandon or April) about Whit and me. It's not that I'm embarrassed, but I want to keep it to myself while it's still new and precious. We also haven't had The Talk yet—the boyfriend/girlfriend talk—and I don't want to be the one who brings it up. I know it's too soon, but the long walks before he went to Texas and the letters that came before the kiss must count for something.

I can see myself losing my virginity to him. Partly because I want to, partly because he makes me feel shiny and special like no one ever has, and partly because I'm ready to just get it over with.

Tuesday, July 23rd

Today is the one-week anniversary of me and Whit getting together. We went on a long walk and talked about writing, and he asked what kind of stuff I write in my diary. I really didn't want to talk about it, so I told him it's boring, just my brain processing the day. He said he doubted that, considering how worried I am about freaking people out, and I probably write all kinds of fucked-up shit.

I was so preoccupied that I didn't notice he was leading us up the driveway of an abandoned house. It was, like, one rainstorm away from sliding down the side of the mountain, but you could tell it was beautiful once. It reminds me of flappers and bootleggers and Citizen Kane—which Whit's never seen.

We climbed in through a window and walked around on buckled wooden floors, under crumbling plaster ceilings. I said that F. Scott and Zelda Fitzgerald might have partied here back in the day.

Later, while making out on the floor in an upstairs bedroom, he whispered that I'm his Zelda.

Did he mean anything by it or was it just a romantic-sounding thing to say? I don't know if it's a compliment. I mentioned that she went crazy and died here, in Asheville, in a fire at a sanitarium. He said he likes it when I'm creepy.

In one room of the house the paint was peeling off the wall in huge sheets, and underneath was this incredible antique wallpaper. It felt like the house was sharing its secret soul with us. Whit used his pocket knife (which he always has because he's a literal Boy Scout) to cut off a piece as a memento.

Wednesday, July 24th

I was tidying up the family film section when it finally happened: Paul came to the store during my shift. He looked the same as always, and he was with his brother Evan, who is a fuckup, but a tall, blond, gym-rat fuckup. I was crouched behind a shelf when they came in, so I had time to collect myself before we came face-to-face.

I was worried he wouldn't speak to me, but when he finally spotted me we both grinned. At the time, I was holding Son of Flubber.

They left, and I realized I forgot to ask Paul if he finished Nuclear Submarine. He said he'd see me around, and I believe him. I'll ask him then.

Thursday, July 25th

I couldn't sleep last night. Even though Paul and I had a nice conversation yesterday, my brain used it as an excuse to screen the highlight reel of That One Infamous Night and made me feel shitty all over again. Then April had a nightmare, and since Mom was at work, I let her stay in bed with me for the rest of the night, even though she kicked me and stole the covers.

I woke up with huge bags under my eyes, which was perfect timing since Whit and I had a date at noon. I tried a trick from Allure where you put spoons in the freezer and use them to bring the swelling down, but I'm not sure it made any difference.

I met Whit in the alley and he drove us an hour out of town and up an unmarked gravel road. His parents are building a house there—they call it their "retreat"—and right now it's nothing but a concrete slab. I wonder if his parents knew he'd taken me there. Do they even know he's dating me? Mom still doesn't.

Whit spread out a blanket and we had cheese and fruit and wine like people in an Impressionist painting. It was so elaborate I was like, "Is he already trying to sleep with me?" But he never made a move. Maybe he'd planned to, but the concrete was hard, and the bugs were buggy, and he reconsidered. Whatever—I was happy just being there with him.

What are you thinking?

Nothing. Just, you're pretty.

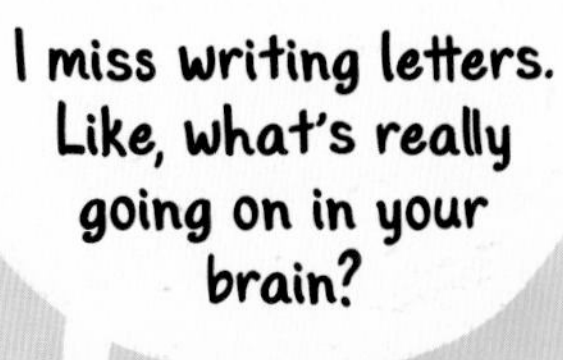
I miss writing letters. Like, what's really going on in your brain?

I'm an open book.

As if! You're inscrutable.

Good word.

What are YOU thinking?
Nothing. Just, you're pretty.

We kissed and sunned ourselves and finished the wine. Whit made up a poem about turkey vultures and ancient mountains and "the curve of Christine's waist" and told me I'm his muse.

The Bele Chere festival is happening this weekend, and we'd talked about going, so I asked if he'd go with me Saturday. He said he's going with his friends on Sunday, but the worst thing was that he didn't invite me. I said it was fine (I have to work on Sunday, anyway) and tried to let it go. It's funnel cakes and shitty bluegrass, not, like, the prom. As Landry would remind me, if she was here, we weren't going out; we were only dating.

On the drive home, a thunderstorm blew up out of nowhere and it rained so hard we had to pull off the road. Whit was looking away when I just blurted it out:

At first I thought he hadn't heard me, and I was like, "Thank God."

But no—he heard me.

Is this because of Bele Chere?

I mean...
kind of.

I really like you, but we just started seeing each other.

And labels make things complicated.

Right.
Totally.
I get it.

And I do. Kind of. But if you're so anti-label, why call me your muse?

Saturday, July 27th

I went to Bele Chere with April and Brandon and Claire and Ashley. We ate curly fries and drank huge cups of lemonade. Ashley spent a long time talking to a girl with a buzzcut at the Earth Now! booth and later told me she's into girls now. I told her that's cool; I don't care who she's into, but it's a relief to know she's not carrying a torch for Whit. I admitted (out of Brandon's hearing) that I'm kind of dating him, and we gossiped about Whit for a while.

Later, I had a pang of missing Landry. It's been a long time since I had someone to talk to about guys and their mysterious ways. But if Landry was still my best friend, I wouldn't be dating Whit.

Sunday, July 28th

Paul came by the store again today. I was alone at the desk watching Drop Dead Fred when the bell jingled on the door and Paul said he thought video clerks were supposed to have impeccable taste.

I said that, yeah, Fred was universally panned, but all the reviewers are old guys who don't know shit about being a girl, and if it was a film about a MAN with an imaginary friend they'd love it. I mean, they gave an Oscar to Harvey!

After watching more of the movie we agreed that I'd come on too strong in favor of Fred. It really was mediocre, but sometimes crappy movies are more inspiring than great ones because they make you think, "I could write that."

Paul was like, "You should write a screenplay! It's easy!"

And I was like, "It can't be THAT easy if you still haven't finished Nuclear Submarine."

But it turned out that he HAD!!! Except for this one new scene he wrote that he's not sure is working. We'd just started talking through it when Whit came in. He was on his way back from Bele Chere and he was extremely sunburnt. He'd brought me a Hawaiian ice, but it melted on the way, and he felt "so bad." I think he was trying to apologize for making plans without me.

I don't think he liked seeing me with Paul. I started telling him how great Nuclear Submarine is and he cut me off because he had "things to do."

I called him after my shift, but he was leaving for dinner with his parents and couldn't talk, so I spent an hour brainstorming screenplay ideas. A girl falls in love with a spirit who can only communicate with her through her Ouija board? Too weird and sad. A girl discovers the reason the guy she's dating doesn't want to get close to her: he's secretly a serial killer. Too dark. I think I'll leave fiction to Paul and Whit and stick to being a muse.

I saw Whit get home with his parents and figured he'd call me back. He didn't. Are we in a fight?

Monday, July 29th

When I left for work, Whit was in the alley smoking gross, skunky pot. I went over and kissed him but it was a very one-sided kiss.

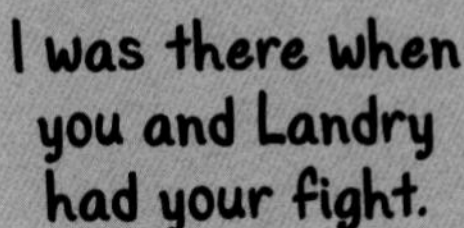

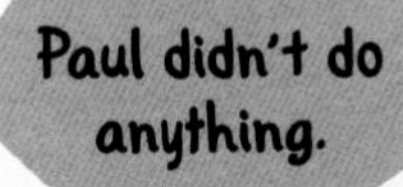

Technically, he didn't. I'm the one who kissed HIM. But anyway...

Tuesday, July 30th

This morning there were flowers on the doorstep and a note in Whit's handwriting.

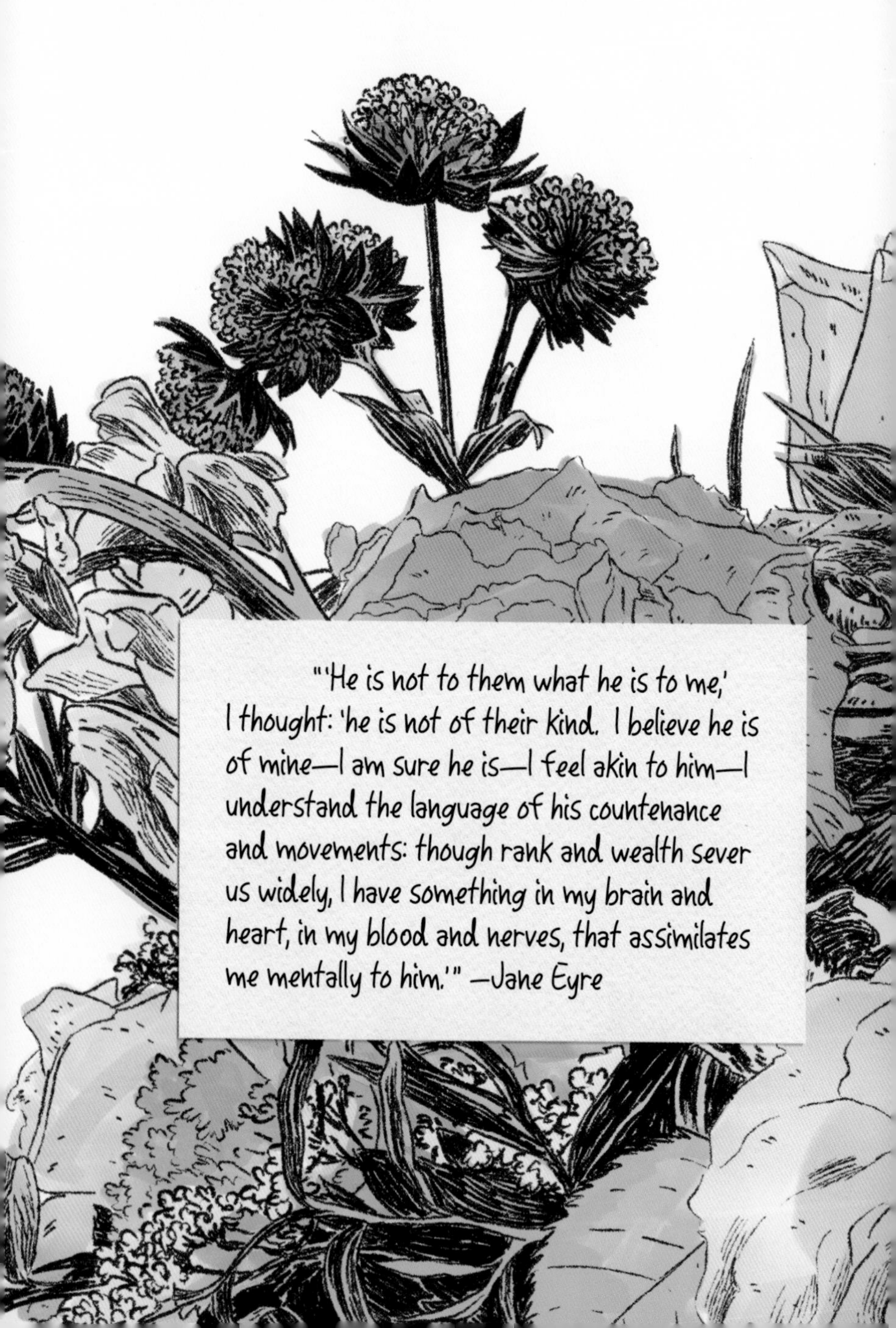

Later, he called and apologized. He said he'd taken me for granted and he was sorry. And would I be his girlfriend?

I didn't want to be the kind of girl who's bought off with romantic gestures, so I said I'd think about it.

Five minutes later, he knocked. Had I thought about it yet? It was very John Cusack in Say Anything. Very Pretty in Pink.

When April asked, in front of Mom, if that was Whit she saw me kissing in the backyard

(by the rusty swing set)

(and the kiddie pool full of dead leaves)

(with his hair still wet from the shower)

I said yeah, it was.

Whit Godwin is my boyfriend.

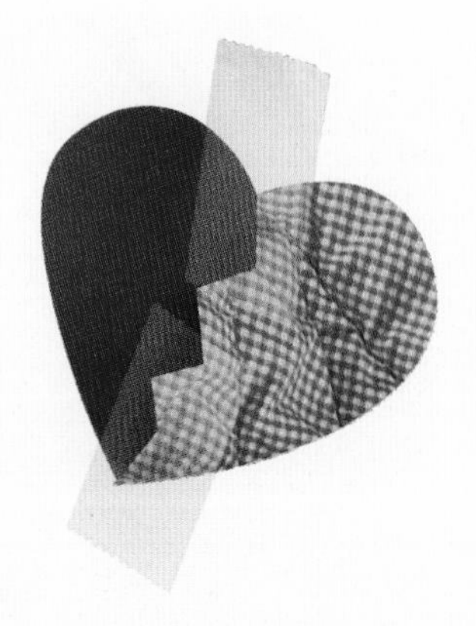

Monday, August 5th

Whit and I went to a baseball game with his friends Kyle and Mel. It was my first double date and it was extremely wholesome. We ate hot dogs and nachos and argued about which team had a more ridiculous name: us (the Tourists) or them (the Crawdads). Whit kept his hand on my knee the whole time.

Mel's on the yearbook committee, which has some crossover with the Chronicle, but she's on a different tier of popularity than me. When we went to the bathroom she told me that she likes me way more than Whit's last girlfriend.

I was like, "You mean Landry?"

"Yeah. He was so into her, but the couple of times I saw them together, he seemed really, like, unsure of himself. And the girl before her—and the one before that—yuck. I don't know where he finds them."

I never felt the need to grill Whit on his dating history, and I still don't, but I had no idea he's gone out with so many girls.

Wednesday, August 7th

Paul came by the store to return some tapes and said Landry was at his work yesterday to buy a sandwich and fish for info about me and Whit. Could it be she realized she fucked up a good thing with both of us?

Of course Paul didn't have the deets, so I filled him in. He's happy I'm happy but reminded me to use protection because who knows what kind of STDs Whit caught from Landry. Ha. But also, he's not wrong.

I asked how things are with JennIFER and what she thinks of his new draft, and he said they're good and he doesn't know what she thinks because she refuses to read the script again until it's totally, 100% finished. Then he pulled out a copy for me! But it's just a loaner; I have to return it when I'm done because he doesn't want it "getting out." Like movie producers are prowling the streets of Asheville, looking for screenplays to steal.

I ripped into it as soon as he left. It's good! There's a new character, Mira, who's the main guy's coworker at the sandwich shop. She's this short brunette who wears baggy jeans and thrifted dresses and is "pretty but doesn't know it." Have I let Whit's muse comment go to my head, or is Mira based on me?

Even if Mira is based on me, it doesn't mean Paul cares about me in more than a friendly way. The last time I read too much into his words, that night I was drunk in the woods and hearing what I wanted to hear, I almost lost him forever.

Saturday, August 10th

It's 1 a.m. and I no longer have a boyfriend. The short version: Whit Godwin is an asshole.

The long version: tonight was Whit's friend's party—kind of our social debut—so of COURSE this was the morning Ashley called me and begged me to go with her to Tennessee. Bele Chere Buzzcut Girl invited her to protest some chip mill across the state line that's clear-cutting old-growth forest, and she was freaking out because she didn't know anyone else who'd be there and what if they all hated her?! I was worried about the party so I got where she was coming from and agreed to go with her. I even changed my shoes because Docs are leather and the Earth Now! people are radical vegans.

Ashley picked me up at 9 a.m. and we headed out. I told her I absolutely had to be back by 6 p.m. because I had a date with Whit, and she promised that wouldn't be a problem. She can't believe she was ever into guys.

Things started out well enough...

But then they took a turn.

Ashley started melting down so I took it upon myself to find us a ride. Mom was at work so I couldn't call her, and Whit didn't answer. But Paul did.

Thirty minutes later he rolled into the parking lot, jazz blasting out his windows. The mechanics all looked at him like he was from another planet.

The whole way back Ashley sobbed about how she's lost her chance to win Buzzcut Girl's radical vegan heart, so Paul dropped her off first. When we got to my house he reminded me I still had his script, so I invited him in.

It was the first time he'd been in my house, and it was weird to see him standing in my room, absorbing the four-foot stack of magazines and the posters and nail polish bottles and miscellaneous detritus of my life. I put on the tape he made me and, because he can't help himself, he started second-guessing the order he put the tracks in. Then we started brainstorming the action scenes in Nuclear Submarine. I had a bunch of ideas for how to stage things. Jamal always talks about how things are shot when we watch movies at work, and I guess some of it sunk in.

We could've talked longer, but an hour had gone by without us noticing, and Paul had work, and I had to get dressed for the party.

Party Outfit
BARETTE; $0 (stolen from April)
Vintage MINIDRESS; $5 at Goodwill
Little silver PURSE; $0 (gift from Mom)
1960s Lucite Cinderella SHOES; $1.50 at Salvation Army

It was a killer look, but I'm developing a theory that the better you look when you walk out the door, the shittier your night will be.

The second I got into Whit's car, I could tell something was off with him, but he played loud rap music all the way to the party so we didn't really talk.

The party was at a big house near the Biltmore Forest Country Club. There weren't many guests—just ten other kids, including Mel and Kyle, and Eric and the girlfriend he went back to instead of dating me, who he seemed very annoyed with—and everyone was hanging in the kitchen. Right away I felt out of place. All the other girls were catalog-model perfect in Levi's and little T-shirts that showed flashes of their perfect flat stomachs. I knew some of them from Asheville High—by sight, anyway—but others were kids from Landry's school. Socially, they were all a cut above me.

A tall girl with spindly eyebrows complimented my "Cinderella shoes," but when I said they were vintage, she told me that her friend got a fungus from secondhand shoes and "I wouldn't risk it."

We went down to the rec room and the guys played pool while the girls drank screwdrivers at the tiki bar. I kept looking to Whit for reassurance, but he was never looking at me.

They started talking about some girl who'd gotten caught sleeping with her physics tutor and sent to an out-of-state boarding school. Then they ragged on a once-hot junior at Asheville High who was prematurely balding.

Then Spindly Eyebrows said she'd just been at a party where Landry got so drunk she passed out in the bathroom and a quarterback had to break the door down. Hearing that made me ill. It sucks to know she's going off the rails. I remembered Mom telling me to reach out to her and how I refused. But who's to say it would have made any difference? Even if I'd been there, could I really have protected her?

Then Mel outed me as Landry's ex-best friend and everyone looked at me with hungry eyes. It made me think of that movie Paul's brother rented. They were the cannibal girls, and I was fresh meat on a platter.

I said, "Landry doesn't need my help wrecking her reputation. She's doing great all on her own." And I excused myself to use the bathroom.

I found a dark room and sat in the corner and wondered what I was doing there. I didn't belong at the party. Eventually I went back downstairs, pulled Whit aside, and told him to take me home.

Why would you bring me to a party and ignore me?
Are you ashamed of me?
You tell me.
I have no clue.
I saw Paul leaving your house earlier.
Oh.
Yeah.
"Oh."

It's not what you think.
Ashley's car broke down and he gave us a ride.
You didn't think to call your BOYFRIEND?
I DID! You weren't home!
Bullshit. I only left for twenty minutes to walk Reggie.
And if you called, why didn't you leave a message?
I didn't know when you'd get it! I had to find someone to come get us so I wouldn't be late for our date!
I'm telling the truth.
Okay?

Paul just came in so I could give him back his screenplay.
For an hour? Yeah, right.
You spied on me for an HOUR?!
Fuck you, Whit.
I don't want to be your girlfriend anymore.

I don't know how to fully express, in words, how I feel right now, so here's a drawing of Whit Godwin being disemboweled by wild dogs.

Sunday, August 11th

So, okay, I retract the disemboweled-by-wild-dogs thing.

Monday, August 12th

The Earth Now! protestors made the front page of the paper! They got arrested for chaining themselves to the gates of that chip mill. I called Ash to tell her we'd dodged a bullet, but she'd already seen the news and was moping about how it would've been "so romantic" to be incarcerated with her crush.

Work tapped me to train our new, blue-haired employee, Star. She was a Jessica until she did acid and realized her name was "preventing her from becoming who she's meant to be," so she changed it and quit school and moved to the mountains to find herself. It occurred to me that she's the Kerouac-type person Whit wants to be. After my shift I went to his house, looked at him in his preppy button-down, and tried to imagine him dropping out of Yale and changing his name to Vikram. I couldn't. But I could see him giving up writing and joining his dad's law firm.

I'm starting to see that our differences aren't a problem; they're the whole reason we like each other. When I look at him, I get to imagine what it must be like to have your life mapped out and locked down. When he looks at me, he imagines the opposite: family tragedy, an after-school job, no clue where I'll end up for school. Maybe he likes sad, complicated girls the same way he likes sad, complicated books. I'm like a sad, complicated book he can kiss.

Tuesday, August 13th

Whit took me to the movies tonight, and afterward, while we were making out in his car, he asked if I've thought about going all the way. I said yeah, but I'm waiting for the right moment. He said he doesn't want to push me, but he's ready when I am. It won't be his first time, but he wishes it was, so it could be with me.

I remember when Landry lost her virginity. She decided she was going to have sex and got, like, laser-focused on it. She called an old boyfriend when he came home from college for Thanksgiving, invited him over to watch a movie, and basically seduced him. He was her nicest ex, so she trusted him to keep his mouth shut. She said the sex wasn't awful, but it did kind of hurt. I wonder if it will hurt for me.

Wednesday, August 14th

School starts in less than a week. Whit and I got our schedules in the mail and we don't have any classes together, not even study hall. My elective is Studio Art and his is Creative Writing, which he says I inspired him to take. The time he and Landry and I saw Fargo, and I was grilling him about what kind of writer he is—it got under his skin. Apparently I was his muse even before we got together.

He was surprised that I'm an artist, not just a writer. I was like, "Artist? Um, no." I like drawing for fun, but my project from art class last year was a Warhol-inspired series of linocut prints featuring

Little Debbie snack cakes. I wouldn't call that art.

He asked if I ever draw people, and would I draw him sometime? I blushed and said I might've drawn him in my diary, and maybe one day I'll show him.

Thursday, August 15th

One of Mom's friends picked her up to go antiquing, so I got to use the car on the condition I take the kiddies shopping for school clothes. Before we left, I gave myself a stern talking-to about my budget. I have a weakness for fall fashion. Those editorials with windswept models running across a prairie in yards of plaid and denim and suede? Irresistible. But for the sake of my future car, I was determined to be frugal.

Before hitting the mall, we went to Beanstreets for sandwiches and iced hot chocolates (the kiddies) and an Americano (me). When we got downstairs with our food, I spotted Paul and JennIFER and Dave and Patchwork Jeans Girl (does she even own another pair of pants?) and went to say hi. JennIFER complimented my hair—always a safe bet when you have nothing to say to another girl—and Patchwork Jeans just smiled.

When April and Brandon and I headed out to the car, Paul caught up with us on the sidewalk and asked if we could talk. I gave Brandon and April the car keys and sent them on ahead.

Once they were out of earshot, Paul told me to be careful with Whit. "JennIFER's in an acting class with some girl who used to date him, and she said Whit's a player."

I was like, no way. If he was dating someone else, I'd know. I live next door.

Paul was like, okay, point taken. Player isn't the exact right term. But Whit has a history of dating freshmen, and girls from other schools, and girls outside his social circle. Girls he can use and discard. Wild girls, like Landry. Damaged girls.

I said, "Is that what I am? Damaged?" He tried to backpedal but I just walked away.

It really pissed me off. He has no clue what he's talking about.

At the mall, I told the kiddies I'd meet them at Sbarro in an hour, stomped into Belk, and bought a Calvin Klein bra set in this sheer black material that made me feel sexy and dangerous and powerful. I'm not the one who needs to be careful; Whit needs to be careful with ME. I'm the one in control. I got mad at him and he sent me flowers. I broke up with him and he came back.

If I didn't know better I'd say Paul was jealous.

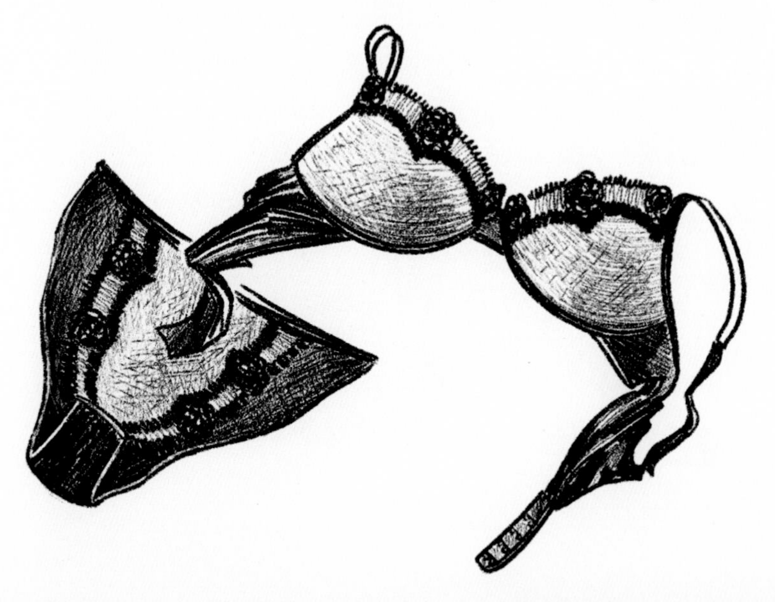

Friday, August 16th

Whit and I were hanging out at his house and I asked if he still plays piano. He said no; his technique is good but over-practice killed any appreciation he ever had for the instrument. He doesn't want the same thing to happen to his writing so he only writes when inspiration strikes.

For a second he looked like he was making up his mind about something, then he was like, "Come with me." He took me down to the basement and showed me a tiny room with whitewashed walls. Inside were a desk, a chair, and an old typewriter—nothing else. He said that a long time ago, when the house was built, it was the maid's room, and now it's his. He's never shown it to anyone else because he likes to keep the space "pure." It's where he's going to write his novel.

He opened a drawer and handed me a story he wrote about a bunch of mountain climbers dying in an avalanche. Whit's dad sent it to his old college roommate, who just happens to be an editor at The New Yorker, and he told Whit he's very talented and he expects it won't be long before he's published in the magazine. I see now why he's so sure of himself—even though the date on the story was two years ago.

I thought, Paul's wrong. Whit's not a creep. It's not possible. He's sweet, and sincere, and he loves me in spite of my flaws. And in that moment I was ready.

We went upstairs and had sex. It wasn't mind-blowing, but it wasn't too painful. My only regret was that it was spontaneous, so I didn't get to show off my new underwear—which is still in a bag with the tags on, anyway.

Afterward, while we were lying there, I thought about how funny it is that Whit hates Paul. If Paul hadn't pissed me off about Whit, I might not have gotten the nerve to go all the way.

Saturday, August 17th

Paul stopped by VideoLife and we talked about the "Top Ten Movies I Watched This Summer" list he's planning for the <u>Chronicle</u>, but the whole time 40% of my brain was going, "Can he tell I've had SEX? Do I seem different? Look different? SMELL different? Do I seem shinier than I used to be?"

I don't feel shinier, or less shiny. I'm just kind of like, this is it? The thing every pop song is about? The thing everyone's trying to protect us from? I mean, it was FINE. I didn't hate it. But what am I missing?

When I got home, Whit brought me a single red rose. It was symbolically obvious and I didn't want Mom to see it and ask questions, so I pressed it between the pages of an old cardiology book of Dad's called <u>The Heart</u>.

Monday, August 19th

Whit and I were hanging out in my room, and my diary was on my desk. He asked to see my drawings of him. I caved and showed him July 16th, when we had our first kiss. He was surprised that I draw "cartoons," but said they're really good. He started turning the page to read more, and when I tried to snatch the book away, he clamped down.

I didn't like how possessive he was acting, but I let him read about the night me and Landry went to the party by the river, and how she got us kicked out of her boyfriend's car. When he finished reading, I told him he was the "nice high school boy" she'd vowed to date. He was like, "Oh, am I?" And he tossed the book aside and pushed me down on the bed.

Saturday, August 31st

Has it really been two weeks since I wrote?! I've been insanely busy with school. The teachers are trying to cram as much into our brains as possible before we all contract senioritis, and I'm the Chronicle's new features editor! It'll look great on college applications, but it's consuming all my free time; I'm in the newspaper office every day at lunch and after school on Wednesdays. The other editors are there, too—including Kayla (sports editor) and Paul (entertainment editor)—but it's hard to have a conversation when you're correcting some freshman's sentence structure.

Things are good with Whit, but we don't see each other much. He drives me to school, and once we sneaked off to make out in the woods behind Enth, but he has cross-country practice in the afternoons and I'm working at VideoLife. We still find time to hang out, though—or at least, to have sex.

I kind of like it now, but I wish he didn't act like we had to do it every chance we got. I'm the one who let that genie out of the bottle, so I shouldn't complain.

I called Planned Parenthood and made an appointment to get on the pill, but they can't see me for a month.

Tuesday, September 3rd

Studio Art kind of sucks. Last year we had an art teacher who put out a bunch of art supplies and left us to our own devices—even let us pick music to play—but he retired and the new teacher, Ms. Adler, is determined to actually, like, teach. Every month is going to be a different unit. First up: fundamentals, which means a lot of rendering spheres with different kinds of lighting. Boring! At least Ashley's there, too.

Whit isn't loving Creative Writing, either. He says Mr. Brooks is "up his own butt" and cares more about students following instructions than doing good work. It's weird, because Paul was in Brooks's class last year and said you could write whatever you wanted, you just had to be smart about it. If the prompt was, "Write a story about a Soviet prison guard" and he wanted to write about a guy who plays Mickey at Disney World, he'd write about a Soviet prison guard who changes careers and gets a job playing Mickey at Disney World.

I kept all that to myself, though. Mentioning Paul would only piss Whit off.

Thursday, September 5th

The first issue of the Chronicle is out tomorrow and all us editors are nervous wrecks. While we were doing the final layout, Kayla and Paul got into it about whether or not to cut a paragraph of football play-by-play.

Friday, September 6th

On the drive to school, I asked Whit if he wanted to hang out after school, before I go to work, but he can't. The team's doing "legs day" and he can't skip it. I got annoyed because it's always legs day or sprints day or long-distance day, and I miss him.

Then I got to school and picked up the Chronicle, my first issue as an editor, and there was a HUGE typo in a headline I wrote, and I felt so stupid I briefly considered resigning in disgrace, but Paul talked me down.

Tuesday, September 10th

I'm so traumatized by Studio Art that I dreamed I was being chased down a tunnel by a smooth white sphere, like that scene in Raiders.

Friday, September 20th

Kayla was heading out after school to cover the cross-country meet at Reynolds, and I decided to go along. I wasn't working, and I'd never been to one of Whit's events, so I thought it would be fun to surprise him.

We sat in the bleachers and Kayla let me look through the zoom lens on her camera—she takes photos, too—and seeing Whit looking all fierce and determined made me feel a swell of pride. Like, yeah, that's MY boyfriend. I liked getting to watch him without him knowing it.

He ended up placing fifth, which seemed good to me, but when I ran over to say hi, he wasn't happy to see me. I went in for a kiss. He pulled back, muttering, "I'm sweaty," and left for a cool-down jog.

The girls ran next, including Ashley, who placed third. She came over and the three of us decided to get food. I said bye to Whit, who was stretching with the other guys, and even though he kissed me this time, I really felt like he was mad at me. I wanted to ask why, but I couldn't with his teammates there.

Kayla and Ash and I went to the new burrito place downtown. I asked them if I fucked up by going to Whit's meet. Isn't that what supportive girlfriends do? Ash said I shouldn't take it personally; Whit's just frustrated that he didn't place higher, especially with me there watching. But I can't help being nervous. I always thought Landry was neurotic when she worried about getting dumped, but I get it now.

Silver lining: if Whit breaks up with me, I don't have to get on the pill. Kayla says the exam involves big metal tools going up your vag, and I'm dreading it.

Saturday, September 21st

Whit caught me in the alley when I left for work in the morning and asked if he could walk me and apologized. It's like Ash thought: he was mad at himself, not at me. He usually places in the top three, and the one time I came to a cross-country meet, he was off his game.

I wish we could've gone out tonight, but he and Kyle had tickets to see Coolio, so I stayed home and baked cookies with Mom and April. I get it, it's Coolio, but I can't help feeling slightly unwanted.

Thursday, September 26th

It's almost the two-month anniversary since Whit and I became boyfriend/girlfriend and he was going to take me out on Saturday, but his parents surprised him with a weekend trip to Yale. They're leaving tomorrow, but he said he'll make it up to me, and I know a two-month anniversary is totally arbitrary, but it sucks.

To add insult to injury, tomorrow's my appointment at Planned Parenthood.

Friday, September 27th

After school, I walked to the clinic and had my exam. The worst part wasn't having my lady parts poked and prodded; it was the half hour I spent in the waiting room, terrified I'd run into someone I knew, and they'd assume I was getting an abortion and spread rumors all over school. Overall, it could've been worse, but it sucks that guys aren't required to undergo the same demeaning rite of passage so they can have sex without mortal terror of getting pregnant.

By the time I got out, my bus was long gone, so I walked the three miles home. When I got back, the pool company's van was in the alley, and a couple guys with permanent tans were closing up Whit's pool. Watching the heavy black cover slide into place felt profound, like part of me is still down there, shimmering in the dark water. Waiting. Hoping. Hungering. I never did tell Whit I swam there when he was away. It's not that I was afraid to, but I wanted to keep that secret for myself.

Monday, September 30th

I don't know if it's the hormones in the pill or what, but last night I had an incredibly vivid dream. I was running down a dark alley...

...with Paul.

And we were being chased. It was like a twisted version of the big action scene in Nuclear Submarine.

I looked down at my hand and I had a gun, too.

Gotcha.
Paul?!
I should've called in sick.
Now I'll have to call in dead.

You're not going to die.
We're in YOUR movie.
You wrote this scene.
You know that's not how it ends.

It's stupid how guilty I feel. It was only a dream, and I only dream-kissed Paul; I didn't dream-fuck him.

Was that imaginary kiss a million times more wonderful than any of the real-life sex I've had with Whit? Yes. Did I cheat on him? No! My boyfriend's out of town, I'm awash in artificial hormones, and my neurons got crossed—that's all. Boys have dreams like this all the time and they don't walk around stewing in guilt and self-reflection, so I won't, either.

Tuesday, October 1st

Whit got home late last night and drove me to school this morning.

I almost cried. In spite of all his mixed signals lately, he sees a future with me—a future beyond high school. Beyond Asheville.

Wednesday, October 2nd

The minimum wage is going up fifty cents! $4.25 to $4.75. I'm so close to having enough for a car that I can almost taste it.

I brought the wage hike up at our editorial meeting and we all agreed that the Chronicle should cover it. The new issue's out on Friday, so we have to submit the files by noon tomorrow. Kayla and I stayed extra late to write the story and redo the whole layout.

While we were grappling with Pagemaker, I mentioned Whit's trip to Yale. Kayla said, no offense to him, but he doesn't seem like Ivy League material. She's in Creative Writing, too, and she said he's always turning things in late or incomplete. Or he'll ignore the prompt and spend more time arguing about his story with Mr. Brooks than he spent writing it in the first place.

I was surprised. He told me he can't write "unless inspiration strikes," but I thought he'd get over that if he had to.

Friday, October 4th

The paper looks great and everyone was talking about our minimum-wage article! A lot of kids didn't even know it was going up. The sophomore whose article we gutted to make room is pissed, but I'm sorry, no one needed his love letter to Ultimate Frisbee.

At work, Jamal told me he's going to make a movie. He thinks if he can get it into some festivals, he can start getting work as a cinematographer. He just needs to find a good script. I was like, "MY FRIEND PAUL HAS A SCRIPT!"

Even though it's an action movie, they could do it super low-budget, like Kevin Smith did with Clerks. I know Paul wanted to direct it himself, but I gave Jamal his number. If it works out, he wants me to be an extra, and he told me to start practicing my "peas and carrots," i.e., what background actors mouth to each other in crowd scenes.

Saturday, October 5th

Tonight, Whit and I had our anniversary dinner. I was late getting home from work, and when I got to my room he was stretched out on my bed with a notebook, working on a story for Creative Writing. I felt kind of weird about him being there—Brandon let him in—but he said being in my space inspires him, and I know he needs a little boost in the inspiration department.

We went to dinner at Magnolia's, and all through the meal he was in a strange mood—keyed-up and hyper. While mutilating the steamed crab on his plate, he told me how writing's hard, and how can he write anything good when his life's been so fucking boring? I'm "lucky" because "real shit" has happened to me. He's "terrified" he won't make it as a writer and he'll have to go to law school after all. I couldn't decide whether to comfort him or give him a light verbal slap, so I just kept nodding and sipping my Pellegrino with lime.

After dinner, we drove to Kyle's house for his birthday party. The usual suspects were there, plus an interloper: Landry. She was in the corner with Mel and Kyle, and they were laughing at something she'd said. Weird, since they constantly shit-talk her.

The second Whit and I walked in, she spotted us and waved. She was acting like, "What breakup? What fight? We're all friends here." I glanced at Whit, unsure what to do, but he conveniently bailed to put our coats in the guest room. Coward.

When I went to the kitchen for a drink, Landry cornered me by the fridge.

I heard about your parents.
I'm sorry.
Don't be. Things are way better since my dad moved out.

My mom spends less time in Xambia, and–
anyway. You're still with Whit!

Yeah. Two months.
You look good together.
Thanks.

I have to go, but it was nice seeing you.
Yeah. You, too.
Don't be a stranger!

I imagined calling and inviting her out with me and Ash and Kayla. The thought was unsettling. Maybe she's changed, though. Maybe she deserves a second chance.

I wandered through the house until I found Whit in the rec room doing birthday shots of Jäger with Kyle. He tried to make me join them, but I hate the taste of licorice, and someone had to drive us home.

Whit was so drunk I was afraid even his hands-off parents would be upset. I still had time before curfew, so I walked him around the neighborhood to sober him up. He kept trying to make out with me, but I was seriously concerned he might puke in my mouth.

He was so wasted he didn't notice I'd steered us past Landry's house. Her car was in the driveway and the light was on in her room. It gave me a warm feeling. I'm not going to call her, though. Not tomorrow, and not ever again.

Sunday, October 6th

I had work at 10 a.m., which sucked, but Whit surprised me in the alley with coffee. I'm annoyed with him about last night, but he and his dad are going to Shining Rock today, and hiking while hungover sounds like punishment enough.

Tuesday, October 8th

Ash and I walked into the art room and the hateful white spheres were gone! But we've started a unit on abstraction, which is almost as bad. Ms. Adler literally had us finger painting to "connect with the materials." What are we, preschoolers?! Kill me.

Wednesday, October 9th

Kayla said Whit wrote a great story for Creative Writing. Even Mr. Brooks said it was remarkable. I called Whit after dinner and said how psyched I am to read his story. He was in the middle of something, but he's going to let me read it tomorrow.

Thursday, October 10th

Whit was all weird and quiet on the drive to school. He's not a morning person, so at first I didn't worry. Then he pulled into his parking space at school and gave me this deadly serious look, and I instantly knew what was coming.

In retrospect, yeah, something was off between us. But how could I ever be sure? Every time he was moody or distant, he'd turn around and talk about me visiting him at Yale, or say how much I inspire him, or bring me coffee.

I spent all day in a fog. I didn't tell my friends, because I knew if I did, I'd cry. And some stupid, desperate part of me thought he'd meet me in the alley and say it was all a mistake, and he loves me after all.

Friday, October 11th

There was no reconciliation in the alley. This is, officially, my second breakup.

At lunch in the Chronicle office, Paul told me that he's letting Jamal direct Nuclear Submarine. For whatever reason, that was the moment I chose to burst into tears and tell him Whit dumped me.

Then I ran off crying like the saddest girl at the eighth-grade dance.

Saturday, October 12th

I've barely stopped crying since lunch on Friday. Yesterday, at work, I even cried to Star. She was like, "Look, it sucks when people give unsolicited advice, but I've had my heart broken a LOT, and there's no better cure than a mosh pit."

So that's how Kayla and Ashley and I ended up watching Star's band play tonight in the basement of a punk house in Montford. I'd never been in a pit before, and at first I was terrified that I'd fall and get trampled, or crushed against the wall. But Star was right—once I became part of that undulating mass of sweaty bodies, nothing else existed. I'd float to the outside of the pit and get pushed back in by the people around the edge, over and over again. It was like catching waves in the ocean. It was like I was a shell being ground into sand by the waves, but I was the ocean, too, and there was no reason to be afraid.

After the show, Kayla and Ash and I chilled in the backyard and talked about college applications and our love lives, or lack thereof. (Ashley finally did hang out with Buzzcut Girl, but she's "seeing someone.") I was sweaty and the cold air felt delicious on my skin, and even though it wasn't an important moment, in the scheme of things, I knew I'd remember it forever.

I sometimes have dreams about finding rooms in my house that I didn't know were there. I'll be in a room I've known all my life, and suddenly there's a door that leads to an attic full of treasures. That's how tonight felt: like a door to a world I might never have known. I'm not over Whit—not even close—but I caught a flash of the other side of heartbreak. Things suck right now, but if I can just hang on, everything will be okay.

Sunday, October 13th

This morning I woke up with a crazy bruise on my arm that I don't remember getting. If you zoom way in, so it's just shades of peach and purple and blue, it's actually kind of beautiful.

Paul came by the store to see if I was still a basket case. I apologized for yelling at him, and he told me it's fine, because he really was thinking the things I suspected he was. Then he handed me a bag of slightly stale chocolate-chip cookies from his work. He's the best.

Tuesday, October 15th

Bruise study I

The materials Ms. Adler meant for us to connect with were paint and charcoal and pastel, not other people's bodies in a mosh pit. And technically, drawing my bruise isn't abstract, it's representational, but I'm not going to tell her that.

Thursday, October 17th

Bruise study II

Tuesday, October 22nd

Bruise study III

Friday, October 25th

Bruise study IV

Monday, November 4th

Whit's dating a freshman—a cheerleader, no less. Kayla, Ashley, and Paul all told me separately. I don't care who he dates. It stings, but between school and SAT prep and the Chronicle, there's no room for heartbreak.

But, like, good luck convincing her to read Vonnegut.

Tuesday, November 5th

We're on to our next unit of Studio Art: landscapes. At least environments are more fun than featureless spheres or pointless splatters. Ms. Adler took us on a field trip downtown to draw buildings, and it made me realize how little I see what's around me, even after living here all my life.

Tuesday, November 12th

Kayla's been using the journalism computer to assemble Creative Writing's fall chapbook. Once a semester they print a booklet with the best story from each student in class and leave it around school for anyone to read, like a tiny literary journal.

I was in the office doing Chronicle stuff, and when she closed the file and left for the day, I went and opened it back up. I knew it was a bad idea, but I couldn't help it—I really wanted to read Whit's story. After all the times he called me his muse, I wanted to know if I'd see myself peering out from between the lines. I did, but not the way I expected.

Lucky

Whit Godwin

Aiden picked me and Jenny up from her house. He was driving a dented Taurus and his friend Ted was riding shotgun. Jenny offered to sit in back with me, but Aiden said absolutely not; she's his "lady." Ted was obviously pissed about having to sit in back with me, Jenny's drag-along guy friend. When he slid in next to me I smelled cigarettes and mildew. He looked weathered, and older–twenties, maybe–and something about him put me on edge.

As we drove to the party, I watched Aiden's hand creep along Jenny's thigh, closer and closer to her crotch. When she said that she and Aiden were good together

It goes on like this for five infuriating pages.

At first, I couldn't wrap my head around it. I knew I'd read those words before, but where? Then the truth hit me: I WROTE those words. I felt an ice-cold hand wrap around my heart and squeeze, and squeeze, and squeeze until I couldn't breathe. But I couldn't stop reading, either.

Whit took my diary entry from March 16th, changed the names, and turned it into the story of "Eric," a dude who follows "Jenny" to a party in hopes of protecting her from her shitty boyfriend. Except when Eric and Jenny are sitting in the church at the end, she tells him he "saved" her and they kiss. Barf.

For all his books, and his private writing chamber, and his New Yorker dreams, the truth is, he has nothing to say. He's not rotten at the core; he's hollow.

The worst part is, I brought this on myself. I didn't want to show him my diary. I knew it was a mistake. I could've said no, but I didn't. He must have copied it that time he was writing in my room.

I can't let him get away with this, but claiming ownership of the story would be even worse. It doesn't take a genius to figure out who "Jenny" is once you know "Eric" is me. I don't want people to think I was a pathetic loser trailing after Landry. Or that we had a drunken makeout session in a church! Well done, Whit. You took a memory that was special to me in so many ways, good and bad, and poisoned it forever.

I can't stop him from writing it, but at least I can tell him to take it out of the chapbook.

Wednesday, November 13th

I tried to corner Whit at lunch, but I couldn't get him alone. Couldn't separate him from the pack. I stayed after school, followed him to cross-country practice, and told him we need to talk. NOW. He asked if I was pregnant. After I said no, he literally ran away from me, because his team was leaving on their run. I yelled for him to call me and he shouted back, "Okay!"

He didn't, though. He doesn't know that I know what he did. Or he doesn't care if I do, because he thinks he's untouchable, and he's right. He has the world at his feet. Every connection; every opportunity. All I have is my thoughts, and words, and drawings. I spent so long convinced they're worthless, but they must have some value if they're worth stealing. What if I'm the thrift-store oil painting that turns out to be, like, a lost Van Gogh? Yeah, I just compared myself to Van Gogh. Sue me.

Thursday, November 14th

I told Kayla that Whit ripped off his story from my diary, and she believed me even before I showed her proof. She'd been surprised when he'd pulled a fully formed story out of thin air.

She and I sat together and checked the story against my diary. He'd copied it almost word for word. We talked for a long time about what to do. I didn't want to go to Brooks, because he'll probably get the principal involved, and they'll call my mom and tell her I went to a rave and was drinking and all that.

Finally, Kayla had the idea to go through and redact everything Whit hadn't written himself. It's perfect: I get to keep my anonymity and Mr. Brooks can see at a glance just how little Whit wrote. He doesn't know how to use Pagemaker, so Kayla's doing the layout and he just approves it. All we have to do is make a copy of the file with our changes, and after Brooks approves the normal version, we give him a disk with the altered version to take to the print shop.

At one point I got cold feet and told Kayla I didn't want to go through with the plan, because I knew we'd get in trouble, but she said she's okay with it if I am. Even though she's just the sports editor, she's serious about journalism and integrity and stuff. And we both want to see Whit squirm.

Here's an excerpt of our handiwork:

Lucky: The Unplagiarized Version

Whit Godwin

Text by Anonymous Redacted

Aiden Jenny

Ted Jenny

Aiden

Ted with me, Jenny's

drag-along guy friend. When he slid in next to me I

After school, Ash and I went downtown. We'd planned to draw buildings for Studio Art, but it was too cold, so we sat in the window at Beanstreets and drew the people walking by. After the past few days, and feeling like the pages of my journal had been violated, it felt good to lose myself in them again.

Wednesday, November 20th

The chapbook file is at Kinko's. I think we actually got away with it.

Thursday, November 21st

Everywhere you look at school, there are piles of blue booklets—which no one's picking up. I was walking down the hall, wondering if anyone would notice or care about my little act of revenge, when Mr. Brooks called me into his classroom. Kayla was there already. Brooks said he wished we'd come to him and asked if I could corroborate my story. I pulled out my diary and showed him March 16th. He stood there for a few minutes, silently turning pages, then handed it back and said it's too bad I'm not in his class, because I'm talented. Maybe I should turn that entry into a short story of my own. Then he gave us two days of detention and said he'd take care of Whit.

I never really believed we'd get away with it, but I thought revenge would make me feel powerful. Instead, I'm filled with doubt. Did I overreact? Should I have tried harder to talk to Whit?

I asked Paul to tell me, honestly, if I'm an evil person. He looked me dead in the eyes and said I'm not. What I did wasn't just about punishing Whit; it was about protecting my soul. It was so exactly what I needed to hear that I burst into tears. He wasn't fazed—this was, like, the fifth time this year I've cried at him—and gave me a lightly crumpled fast food napkin to dry my eyes.

Saturday, November 23rd

Mom ordered takeout from Peking Garden, and after my shift at work I went across the street to pick it up. I was sitting in front of the fish tank, waiting for our food, when I heard Landry's voice on the other side. She wasn't talking to me—she couldn't have known I was there—but she was LOUD. And she was drunk. My heart sank. What happened to not drinking?!

Hey! Waitress! Turn it up!

Um, Landry? Look out for the—

CRASH

Miss, I need you to leave. You're disturbing the other customers.

Relax. I'll pay for that.

Please leave, or I'm calling the police.
Th-that's not necessary!
She's just having a bad reaction to her, uh, medication.
And we're leaving. Okay, Landry?
Um, no. We're staying.
If they call the cops, I'll call the health department and report this shithole for—
Yes, hello, Officer. This is Melissa at Peking Garden—
Fuuuuuck yooou!
Shut up, Landry!
I'm sorry, ma'am. We're going.

Landry didn't see me when she whooshed past, through the glass door to the parking lot. Her pupils were so big and dark, her eyes looked black, but I'm sure that was just her "medication."

The girl with her—a preppy brunette I've seen around, but don't know by name—hung back to slip the manager cash and excuses: Her parents are getting divorced. She's struggling. It won't happen again.

When I saw Landry at that party, I believed the drunk, wild girl I knew really was gone forever. Part of me even thought I could take some credit: that without me there to cover for her, she hit rock bottom and started to swim back up. But now I see it's got nothing to do with me. She's swinging through the world like a wrecking ball, and nothing I do will change her trajectory. All I can do is keep out of the way.

The hostess appeared with my food, and I went home and ate kung pao chicken with my family. We took turns opening fortune cookies and reading the messages inside, but when I opened mine, it was empty. Mom said an empty fortune cookie is the luckiest kind of all, and I believe her.

I used to think Landry was the lucky one, but there's no way I'd trade places now. Not for all the money in the world.

Sunday, November 24th

When I got to work, the first words out of Jamal's mouth were, "Hey. Talked to Paul lately?" I said not since Friday, and why did he ask? He said, "Oh. Never mind," and speed-walked into the back to rewind tapes. Is he hiding something? Is Paul okay? Are he and Jamal having creative differences over Nuclear Submarine? God, I hope not.

I opened Paul's rental history and looked for clues to his mental state. Last week he rented the saddest movies ever, Kids and The Elephant Man. Did that double dose of tragedy push him over the edge?

Or maybe he's slogging through the same nightmare as me and the rest of our class. Our futures are riding on our GPAs, our SAT scores, and where we go to college. I haven't even sent in my applications, but I'm already panicking about whether to study journalism, English, or mass communication. What if I pick the wrong major and my career's DOA?! Mom wants me to relax, because, "College is about finding yourself," but why does finding myself have to be so expensive? The whole thing feels like a scam.

I'm constantly fantasizing about finally getting my own car, driving away, and never coming back. Maybe I'll say, screw college, and go out west to live out a Tom Petty song. I'll get a job at a diner on Route 66 and work my way up to buying the place. Every so often I'll serve a cheeseburger to someone I used to know, but they won't recognize me—and that's exactly how I like it.

Tuesday, November 26th

Here's a sketch for my big landscape piece in Studio Art. Everyone else is drawing mountains and waterfalls, stuff you'd see in a doctor's office waiting room, but I was staring out the window at VideoLife and I had an epiphany: landscapes don't have to be pretty. They don't have to be about aesthetics. Like, why not an autobiographical landscape?

The view from the job I begged my mom to let me take. The gas station I saw get robbed over the summer. The Chinese restaurant where my ex-best friend made a drunken scene. It might look like nothing, just an ordinary commercial corner, but it's a place I never want to forget.

Thursday, November 28th

It's lame that we still celebrate a holiday based on genocide, but at least the food's good. Mom got up at the crack of dawn to start the turkey. My only job was to make the cranberry sauce, but I somehow burned it. I got the last can of jellied cranberry at Ingles, which was dented, and as I was trying to remember if dented cans really do cause botulism, I glanced down the aisle and saw Whit.

He was walking toward me, and he looked mad.

Hey.
Happy Thanksgiving.

Um, how are you?

Not great.
Brooks failed me.
My GPA's trashed.
My dad lost his shit.
That sucks. I'm sorry.

I just wanted you to know that my dad talked to admissions at Yale and they're going to overlook it.

So all you accomplished was proving to the world what a vindictive bitch you are.

I'd rather be a bitch than a coward.

You said you wanted to be free of your Dad's expectations.
You said I'm lucky 'cause I've lived through "real shit."
But the second things get real for you, here comes Daddy to save you.
I'm sure you'll go to Yale, and I'm sure you'll be a great success in life.
But you'll never be a real writer.

Back at home, the turkey wasn't done, and my heart wouldn't stop pounding, so I went to the upstairs bathroom and cut off all my hair.

Monday, December 2nd

Mom insisted on taking me to fix my hair at the JCPenney salon, and now it's even shorter. Kayla asked if I was having an "episode," but Paul said I look like Jean Seberg in Breathless.

I was like, "Oh yeah, you had that whole French New Wave phase over the summer." Then I casually asked if something's going on with him, 'cause his rentals have been BLEAK.

He laughed and asked if I always stalk his account, and I said it's his fault for having such great taste. He didn't answer my question, though. If there really is something going on with him, why would he tell Jamal and not me?

I hope I'm not out of his inner circle. He's back to being one of the people I can turn to when I need help. I wish he'd let me be that person for him, too.

Tuesday, December 3rd

We turned in our landscape projects today and HELL YEAH, we're starting on self-portraits! Even Ms. Adler seemed excited that all the boring shit was behind us. Our warm-up exercise was drawing pictures of ourselves with our eyes closed, and thinking about the ways we each see ourselves in our mind's eye. The pictures looked Picasso-y, with everyone's eyes and noses floating off their faces, but it was cool how much they looked like us. It's not a "good" drawing, but it's my favorite picture I ever drew of myself.

Wednesday, December 4th

This morning before school I opened the newspaper and there she was: a burgundy Honda Accord hatchback with AC, cruise control, and 120k miles for a very reasonable $2,100.

I'm only $400 short, so I showed Mom the ad, but she just smiled vaguely and said maybe it'll still be available in a couple of months, i.e., "No way am I loaning you the money."

Paul had to skip the after-school <u>Chronicle</u> meeting so he could cover someone's shift at work, so he just missed JennIFER dropping by to return a sweatshirt of his. She almost never comes by the office, so I pointed her to Paul's desk. She said she loves my new hair, and that "most girls" wouldn't be brave enough to cut it that short. I'm delighted to see she hasn't lost her touch for backhanded compliments.

Saturday, December 7th

I took the SAT this morning. The kid in front of me had a twelve-inch rat tail, which was extremely distracting, but I still finished the test early. All the SAT guides say it's bad to finish with lots of time left, but on the other hand, you aren't supposed to second-guess your answers because you're more likely to get them wrong. The SAT catch-22.

After the test, Mom picked me up and said she was taking me to celebrate, but refused to reveal our destination. We went east to Swannanoa, then drove around until I pointed out some emus. She instantly did a U-turn. "They said if I saw emus, I'd gone too far." I was like, okay, but who is "they"?!

We bounced down a potholed gravel drive until we reached a farmhouse covered in tattered prayer flags. There, parked in the yard, was a burgundy '85 Honda Accord hatchback.

I felt dazed as Mom and I walked toward the car. A white-haired Willie Nelson type came down from the porch, and we drove the Accord around the back roads while Mom grilled him on mileage and maintenance and ownership history. When we got back to the farmhouse, she asked if I liked the car. She's going to cover the amount I'm missing and call it an early graduation gift.

I hugged her and started to cry.

After we went to the bank and the title office and put new plates on the car, Mom went home and I drove to the sub shop downtown to show Paul my new ride. I got a parking spot right outside, but even though I know he works Saturdays, he wasn't there.

On the off chance he'd roll in soon, I bought a chocolate chip cookie, like he brought me when I got dumped, and sat down with a copy of Mountain Xpress. I was the only customer, and my powers of invisibility must've been fully engaged, because the girls behind the counter made zero effort to keep their voices down.

Brandy?
Yeah?

Does my tongue piercing look infected?
Ew! I don't need to see that!

CRUNCH
Show it to Paul. You know you want to, and he's single again.
!?

Paul is single.

Paul is single.

Paul is single and he never told me.

I went back to my car and cried for the second time today. Paul is single and everyone knows it but me. Jamal knows—that's why he's been acting cagey. Infected Tongue Piercing knows. Why didn't he tell me? And why do I care so much?

The answer burst out of my heart in a glitter-cloud sucker punch of rom-com cliché: I'm in love with Paul.

I love his weird jazz mix tapes. His smelly car. His ugly shirts. His video rental history has all the depth and nuance of the great works of literature, and I would read a thousand drafts of Nuclear Submarine because every one is fun and weird and special in some unexpected way. He's unique, and uncategorizable, and every time I said he wasn't my type I was lying to myself.

Everyone but me could see the truth—the only logical reason Paul didn't tell me he and JennIFER broke up is that he doesn't like me back. All this time I told myself I was out of his league when the truth was that he's out of mine.

I allowed myself ten more minutes of self-pity, then wiped my eyes and started the car. I drove along the river, past the creepy abandoned prison, and up Beaucatcher Mountain. I went under Helen's Bridge. I got a Frosty at Wendy's, where the cute drive-through guy recognized me—even with my new hair and without Landry—and complimented my new wheels. I watched the sun set at Beaver Lake. Then I drove home.

I was listening to the college station, and as I pulled into the driveway they played an amazing song. It was a mix of spooky, sexy, and sad that gave me chills, and the singer had a voice like Billie Holiday. I sat in the driveway and hoped the DJ would come on and say who the artist was, but as the minutes ticked by I asked myself how long I wanted to sit there, running down my battery.

The DJ isn't going to say the name of the song.

The boy I love isn't going to love me back.

I cut the motor and went inside.

Tuesday, December 10th

Kayla and Ashley and I went to Beanstreets after school to work on our college essays, but all we did was overcaffeinate and gossip. Ash had run into Buzzcut Girl on the sidewalk and fallen for her all over again, and Kayla was convinced the barista with the Buddy Holly glasses was flirting with her. I was grateful they were too obsessed with their own love lives to bother asking about mine.

Friday, December 13th

It's always jarring when teachers show up at my job and I'm forced to remember they're humans with lives, not robots who sleep in the maintenance closet at school. But when Mr. Brooks came in today, it was a whole new flavor of weird. He saw me shelving new releases and asked if I ever wrote that story. I was like, nah. Fiction isn't my thing.

But it was dark when I got home, and while passing Whit's car in the alley, I realized he and his baby freshman girlfriend were inside, making out. After I went inside, I sat down and wrote five pages about the two of them getting attacked by a lover's lane serial killer. I killed Whit, but I don't really have anything against his girlfriend, so I let her live.

It's not high art, just a dumb slasher story, but maybe Brooks is right, and I have fiction in me after all.

Saturday, December 14th

Ashley and I were supposed to sleep over at Kayla's tonight, but Kayla got sick and the plan fizzled. I decided this was my chance to take another stab at writing. I set out a new notebook, and a new Pilot pen, and a Heath bar, and a cup of tea, and then I was out of stalling techniques, so I sat down.

I thought I'd try and write my own fictional version of March 16th, like Mr. Brooks suggested, and it would flow out of me the way it did last night, but I couldn't even nail the first line. I crossed out one after another until, finally, I ripped out the page. I was like, what's wrong with me? Am I a psycho who can't write anything but sadistic revenge fantasies?!

To calm my brain down, I sketched out the scene in my head: a car driving down a two-lane road at night. Then I drew the girl in the back seat of the car. Her name was Jamie. Her friend Alison, and Alison's boyfriend, Tom, and Tom's drug dealer were there, too.

I kept going that way, picture after picture. It was less like I was making up the story and more like I was a camera following Jamie, documenting everything she did, and saw, and every emotion that crossed her face. At first it felt the same as drawing a scene from my own life, because Jamie's a lot like me, but when I draw stories about myself, I know how they end. When Jamie lost track of Alison at the warehouse party, I realized this was different. Jamie was standing in the dark, with nothing but questions, and I was, too.

Was Alison in danger? Was she kissing Tom on the hood of a car, or did she fall in the river and drown? Did someone push her? Was this story a mystery? A comic-book mystery? Is that even a thing? Is it totally stupid and misguided, or am I going to be the S. E. Hinton of comic books?

Is this how writing screenplays feels to Paul?

I drew as fast as I could, faster than I ever had, because the story was moving through me like lightning, and each question I answered revealed a new question. I'd have kept going forever, drunk on the rush of discovery, if my hand hadn't started to ache.

When I finally put the pen down, I was sweating like I'd run for miles. I opened the window and stood there in my T-shirt with the icy December night washing over me. Across the alley, the light was on in Whit's room, and I silently thanked him. For dumping me. For showing me I'm so much better than him. If he wasn't such a piece of shit, I might not have found my way to writing this story at all. In his own obnoxious way, he's my muse, too.

Monday, December 23rd

I've been neglecting my journal. I can't help it: I'm in the throes of new love...with my comic book. I think about it all day at school and work on it when I get home, which means I don't have time to write in here, too. But yesterday I wrote Jamie into a corner, so until I get her out of it, here I am.

Today was the last day of class before winter break. I picked up my graded self-portrait final—I took a chance and made a drawing of my hands, not my face—and Adler gave me an A for "technical skill and thinking outside the box." Then, at lunch, all the Chronicle editors had a pizza party. Paul and I talked about weird Christmas movies, and he was going crazy trying to remember the name of one his parents rented when he was a kid. It was about Santa, an amusement park, and a giant rabbit. I promised to look for it at VideoLife. I doubt our system goes back to the '80s, and Paul says his parents haven't rented with us since Blockbuster opened, but it's worth a try.

Things have felt normal-ish between me and Paul. He still hasn't admitted he's single, and the little voice in my head that longs to kiss him is starting to quiet down. But driving home this afternoon, I pulled up next to him at a red light. We were singing along to the same song on the radio, and when we saw each other, we both cracked up. How can I get over a guy who loves jazz AND knows all the words to "Just a Girl" by No Doubt? If I don't tell him how I feel, I'll regret it for the rest of my life. Even if he breaks my heart, I have to tell him. I just don't know how.

Tuesday, December 24th

My SAT score came: 1460! I finished my college applications and walked them down to the mailbox on the corner. The last time I mailed something here, it was a letter to Whit.

I applied to UNC-Chapel Hill, UNC-Asheville, and NC State. I'll go with whichever school gives me the most money, and if I really hate where I end up, I can always transfer.

I worked the afternoon shift, which was busy—lots of families coming in for seasonal rentals; lots of "cool" guys informing me that Die Hard is a Christmas movie. Eventually it slowed down enough that I had time to check our records for the movie Paul was trying to remember. It turns out our records go back to 1986! And even though his parents stopped using their account, they're still in the system.

As I scrolled through the far reaches of Paul's family's rental history, I had an epiphany. I knew how to achieve my Say Anything moment, my version of standing outside his house, blasting "In Your Eyes" from a boom box. There's something I can give him that no one else can.

I went home and worked on it for hours and hours. It's kind of a lot—I know that. But even if he doesn't love me, I know it won't be wasted on him. He'll treasure it forever. Every time he looks at it, he'll remember me.

Wednesday, December 25th

It's Christmas. We ate cookies for breakfast and opened presents and played Monopoly. I was really feeling the holiday spirit, so I teamed up with Brandon and saved him from bankruptcy. After lunch we went to see Jerry Maguire, and it was good, but all I could think about was how I'm scheduled to work tomorrow and Paul has videos due.

Thursday, December 26th

My heart stopped every time someone put a tape through the return slot, but it was never Paul. This is like the first time he's ever been late returning a rental. Is this a sign that I shouldn't give him his gift? Should I put it on the top shelf in my closet and pretend I never made it? Ughhh. I don't know, I don't know, I don't know.

Saturday, December 28th

Last night started off in a typical way. April and Brandon were both sleeping over with friends, and Mom was having dinner with Eileen at some new health-food place, and I was home alone, vegging in front of the TV. Then I remembered: I have a car! I can LEAVE!

I put on makeup and a techno-beatnik outfit—black mock turtleneck; ripped black tights; silver skirt that zips up the front—and drove to Beanstreets to drink coffee and work on my comic book. Just as I sat down, Jamal walked in.

He said he was meeting Paul to talk about Nuclear Submarine and I barely had time to be nervous because the door was already opening and Paul was walking in. Jamal went to the counter to buy a coffee, and Paul came over to me. I looked him straight in the eye and said:

And, um, actually–
Hey, man–
I hate to bail, but I just got paged. They need me at the store.
It's cool. I'll call ya.
Actually what?
Um...
I made you something.
Oh my God.
Christine.
Is this what I think it is?

If you think it's a comprehensive list of every film you and your family ever rented at VideoLife, then yeah.

Merry Christmas, Paul.

This is seriously the best gift ever.
I have something for you, too.
A mix tape.
But it's not done yet.

Will it ever be?

Next month. February at the latest.
Um, Paul?
There's something I need to ask you.

Why didn't you tell me you and Jennifer broke up?
You know?
I overheard your coworker. The one with the tongue piercing?
Fucking Shana.
Are you dating her?
NO!
Okay... then why the secrecy?
I was just... trying to put some space between the breakup and...
and, um...
Can I take you somewhere? Now?

PARK
This is where I come when I need to think.
LEVEL 7

So.
So...
Ugh. There's nothing more obnoxious than Christmas carols after Christmas.
Aw, Paul, you're such a Scrooge.
Siiilent night, hoooly night...
I'm really not! I'm cool with them BEFORE Christmas, I just—
Look, there's Landry.

It's weird how people are this huge part of your life and one day they're just...not.

Yeah.

Um, anyway...
Did I tell you I started a new screenplay?
It's like Time Bandits meets—

I started a book!

Wait, like, you're writing one?

Not, like, a real book. A comic book.

Can I read it?
I won't steal it. I mean, probably.

Haha.
God, Paul. I'm going to miss you next year.
Our talks, and, um–
everything else.
Me too, Christine.
Really?
Yeah.
So much.

Is this okay?
Okay?
Don't be stupid, Paul.

It's perfect.

Monday, December 30th

Paul said he's been in love with me for a long time, but he didn't think I felt the same. That's my fault—I kissed him and said I didn't like him like that, and he never forgot it.

But everything's different now. I'm bringing him to Star's band's show on New Year's Eve, and we're going to kiss at midnight and send this whole crappy year off in style. I feel tingly whenever I think about it.

I let him read my comic book—even the parts that suck—and he loved it, mostly. He had thoughts, and it's weird to be the one getting feedback from him instead of the one giving it, but it feels right.

Everything about Paul feels right. Every kiss is like the first one—or better, since I'm not drunk off my ass and he doesn't have a girlfriend.

I mean, aside from me. We talked about it and we both agreed it would be weird not to make it official. I told Ash and Kayla, and they were like, "About freaking time!"

I couldn't wait to tell Mom, either. I guess that when my boyfriend's as wonderful as Paul, I can't keep my big mouth shut.

Tuesday, December 31st

It's almost 1997—almost time to put this journal away and start a new one—and I haven't decided on my New Year's resolution. I'm not sure I'll make one. I think, on this at least, I agree with Landry: they're stupid. They were probably invented by someone in advertising to make us spend a bunch of money on gym memberships and self-help books. The whole idea of time was probably invented to make us feel like we're falling behind from the moment we're born.

I have no idea where I'll go to college, or if Paul will break my heart, or if I'll ever get out of this town. God, I'd fucking better. But me, here, now—it's not so bad. Am I happy? I don't know. I'm not, like, singing in the streets. But when I think about my life, the one thing I know for sure is that I'm not ready for this moment to end.

Acknowledgments

Thank you to Tamara, Raj, Whitley, Chris, Jason Sandford, and other locals, current and former, for sharing stories from their misspent youths and helping me get the details of "old Asheville" right. Everyone on ST—you know who you are—for moral support. Julia Wertz, for letting me borrow her handwriting for Landry. The North Carolina room at Pack Memorial Library. Sean Michael Robinson for his razor-sharp memories of working in a high school newsroom. Patti Glazer of Glazer Architecture for sharing photos of Peking Garden restaurant, which I'd almost despaired of finding. Malaprop's Bookstore, the heart of downtown since 1982. My wonderful husband Aaron, my daughter PJ, and my parents and mother-in-law, who provided the childcare that allowed me to complete this book. My agent, Judy Hansen, for her encouragement and support. And most of all, my deepest gratitude to my editor Margaret Ferguson, who gave me a chance to make this messy, complicated book and wouldn't let me give up when I wanted to. Without her brilliant insights and guidance, I couldn't have found my way to the other side.